PIERCED

SYDNEY LANDON

Aidan
Copyright 2016 – Sydney Landon

Cover Design and Interior Format – The Killion Group

ACKNOWLEDGEMENTS

A special note of thanks to my wonderful PA Amanda Lanclos.

A thank you to Kim Killion with Hot Damn Designs for the wonderful cover. And to my editors: Marion Archer and Jenny Sims with Editing4Indies. Love you ladies!

And to my blogger friends, Catherine Crook with A Reader Lives a Thousand Lives, Jennifer Harried with Book Bitches Blog, Christine with Books and Beyond, Jenn with SMI Book Club, Chloe with Smart Mouth Smut, Shelly with Sexy Bibliophiles, Amanda and Heather with Crazy Cajun Book Addicts, Stacia with Three Girls & A Book Obsession, Lisa Salvary and Confessions of a Book Lovin Junkie.

CHAPTER ONE

Aidan

I look around the outdoor beach bar as I ponder the latest email from my father. I know he's not telling me something. Of course, I can't really blame him, considering I left town almost a year ago and haven't been back since. You don't do that kind of shit when you're an only child. But I couldn't stay. When the woman you thought was the love of your life since childhood dies and you do nothing to save her, it tends to fuck you up in the head a bit. So yeah, as soon as my best friend, Lucian Quinn, married Lia and promptly popped out a kid on their wedding night, I'd taken off.

I didn't have a particular destination in mind when I left Asheville, North Carolina, but when I stopped for gas in Charleston, South Carolina, I decided to stay the night. And I never left. I rented a house right on the ocean, spending my days wandering around in the tide and my nights drinking far too much. I also fucked my way through most of the women vacationing in the area. I know what you're thinking: How could I sleep with someone else so soon after losing the woman I professed to love? First off, no sleeping was involved. It was straight fucking—hard—and then I'd show them the door. No strings, no feelings, no flowers. Instead of considering me a lousy bastard, look at it as me simply trying to avoid dealing with the shitshow I call my life.

Unfortunately, as it often happens, life has intruded on my frat-boy existence. My mother is sick, and my father is being as evasive as a dirty politician up for re-election. I know she hasn't been feeling well for the last month, and she's had some tests run, but that's about as much as anyone's told me. Since I've cut off most contact with my friends, I can't really blame anyone other than myself for the fact that I'm three hundred miles from home and have no fucking idea what's going on. Wasn't that the way I wanted it? Hell, I laid down that law when I left. I gave Lucian and my father my new email address, instructing them both it was for emergencies only, and I hadn't looked back.

Truthfully, I didn't miss anyone for months. I'd been too mired in my own misery to wonder about the outside world. I received regular messages from both Luc and my father, and sometimes I replied, but more often, I didn't. Lucian and I had been friends since grade school. We'd been quite a pair. He was the brains of the outfit, and I was the comic relief. Then Cassie Wyatt came along, and there were three of us.

I was crazy in love with Cassie from the first, but Luc had always been it for her, and that never changed. As in all famous love stories, theirs was eventually mired in tragedy and death. Cassie struggled with mental illness, and when she got pregnant during college with Luc's baby, things took a turn for the worse. We were sharing an apartment, and despite my infatuation with her, even I'd noticed her increasingly erratic behavior. I was afraid being off her bipolar medication would send her into a tailspin, and my fears were justified.

I was in the habit of staying out late most nights just to avoid the almost daily fights between Luc and Cassie. On the night our lives changed forever, I'd gone home early.

I'd been restless that evening and not really in the mood for the endless partying that had become so much a way of life. I figured I'd make some excuse about not feeling well and go straight to my room. With that plan in mind, it had been rather anti-climactic to find a quiet apartment when I arrived home. I had grabbed a glass of water and was walking down the hallway when I heard a muffled shout, followed by laughter that seemed eerily sinister.

I hesitated in front of their closed door for a moment. The last thing I wanted was to walk in on them having sex. I had almost decided to move on when something stopped me. The air was so heavy around me that I was having difficulty taking a full breath. I felt on the edge of a panic attack, and I had no idea why. All I knew was that every internal alarm was blaring, and almost in slow motion, I reached out to open their door. In the hours following that moment, I would wonder why I hadn't at least knocked first. What made me barge in without extending that common courtesy?

Then the world had fallen away only to slam back into focus as I had attempted to process the horrifying scene before my eyes. *Blood*—so much blood everywhere. For precious seconds, I'd been transfixed by the crimson splashes against the pale color of the sheets. I honestly didn't know what finally prompted me into action. Somehow, I called 9-1-1. The sound of Lucian choking and gasping and Cassie expelling some kind of broken, demented laughter has haunted me ever since. Out of the pieces I remember, I think those two things might be the worst. For the most part, I blocked them from my mind during my waking hours, but at night, they often slipped in when my guard was down.

Of course, now I had new horrors to add to the fucked-up slideshow in my head—Cassie trying to kill Lucian's pregnant girlfriend, Lia. I tried to save them both, but in the end, Cassie didn't let that happen. Realistically, I'd come to accept that Cassie's life had always been destined to end tragically. By saving her the first time, I simply delayed the inevitable. *That's the benefit of hindsight as they say.* You can't cheat death, though, especially when one person is determined to dance with it at every opportunity. It didn't make it any easier to accept, but that's where the alcohol and women came into play. On the days when I've been too close to the edge, I did and still do whatever's needed to dull the pain.

I'm swallowing the last of my Dewar's scotch when I see her walk past. My hand freezes, holding the glass suspended in midair before I slowly lower it back to the table. Her hair is dark—almost black—but that's not what has my attention. Even from a distance, she looks familiar. Then it hits me. *Lia.* Outside of the dark hair, she bears an uncanny resemblance to Lucian's wife. Lia is a blonde, and there's no reason she would be here. I've never known Luc to vacation in this particular area.

I've almost written it off as everyone having a twin somewhere when she turns in my direction and our eyes meet. In that split second, I see it. She recognizes *me.* I'm not even sure how that's possible. I look nothing like my normally well-groomed self. My hair is longer than it's ever been and curls in a way that would bug the hell out of me if I gave a good damn. I'm wearing shorts and a faded T-shirt instead of a suit, and I'm sporting way too much facial hair since I haven't shaved in days.

She appears hesitant, as if she's second-guessing herself. Then she runs what looks like a self-conscious hand over her dark locks before making her way to me slowly. Despite myself, I'm intrigued. She stops several feet away and studies me uncertainly. Up close, she'd almost be a dead ringer for Lia. Then realization strikes at almost the exact moment she opens her mouth to speak. *Kara Jacks, Lia's cousin.*

"Aidan?" she murmurs softly. She's wearing a long, flowing dress that blows in the breeze, and the glow of her skin indicates she too has been here longer than a few days.

"Kara," I say confidently, as if I hadn't just figured out who she was a split second earlier. I get to my feet and then wonder what to do. I've seen her a few times, but we're merely acquaintances. It seems ridiculously formal to shake her hand but a bit too personal to hug her. Instead, I put my hands in the pockets of my shorts and rock back on my heels. I haven't had to put this much thought or effort into conversation since I left Asheville, and I feel awkward as hell. I must admit, that's a first for me. Charming the ladies has been second nature to me since I was old enough to appreciate the difference between the sexes. I can't seem to find any of that ease right now, though. She's looking about as uncomfortable as I feel. Clearing my throat, I add, "It's good to see you again. How long have you been here?"

She shrugs her slim shoulders before saying, "A couple of weeks. I'm staying at Uncle Lee's place just down the beach." She points in the opposite direction from my rental house. "How about you?"

I find it hard to believe she hasn't heard through her family connections that I've been AWOL for a year, but I decide to let it go and simply answer with a vague, "A while," instead. I don't feel like socializing, but I find myself asking, "Would you like to sit down and have a drink?" I feel certain she'll say no, as it's obvious she's ill at ease.

Therefore, I'm surprised when she steps up to my table and pulls out a chair. "Sure, it would be nice to have some company for a change." She's already seated, and I'm still standing. Fuck, why did I have to revert to being a gentleman? At best, this will probably be thirty minutes of awkward and strained conversation.

I take my seat. "What would you like?"

She looks me in the eyes for the first time, and I feel a funny catch in my chest. Her resemblance to Lia makes me homesick for my friends. But something else is there as well. She has the type of familiar haunted look I see in the mirror every day. I find myself wanting to fix whatever's bothering her, which is a fucking joke since I can't even deal with my own problems. It takes me a minute to realize she's said something. "Sorry," I mutter. "I didn't catch that."

The polite expression falls away, and she gives me a genuine smile. *Fucking beautiful.* I stare, mesmerized by the transformation. She's almost glowing now as mischief dances in her eyes. *You're playing with fire, sweetheart.* I damn well know she's not one of my usual evening partners, but my hard cock isn't getting that memo. She chuckles, which makes it even worse. "I said I'll have whatever you're having. The chick drinks make me sick."

I hold my glass up, shaking the melting ice cubes together in the bottom of it. "You do know this is scotch, right? Maybe we should start you with something a bit tamer."

She seals her fate when she says, "Bring it on, Spencer. I promise I can handle it." *Well, fuck.* My dick is no longer listening to reason. He wants what he wants, and that's the woman sitting in front of me looking equal parts college girl and temptress. I motion for Charlie, the bartender, and hold up two fingers. Since I'm usually here at some point each evening, he and I have developed our own sign language. He knows what I want without me putting forth the effort of opening my mouth, and I reward him with a big tip at the end of the night. If only all relationships could be so simple.

Kara surprises me when our drinks arrive. Instead of sipping the scotch, she throws it back. Her eyes water for a moment, but that's her only visible sign of discomfort. Damn, I've known many grown men who couldn't shoot scotch without cringing. I tap a hand to my forehead giving her a salute. "Very impressive," I say and mean every word. Hell, it's a proven fact I've always been a sucker for a crazy woman. Instead of waiting for me, she holds her empty glass up and signals Charlie to refill it. I'm in the middle of taking another sip when she says bluntly, "So you're running away too?" Shrugging at my surprised expression, she adds, "Don't bother to deny it. You know how families talk. Everyone's worried about you at home. I personally figured you were in a cave somewhere roughing it." Then she gives a lazy perusal of my body. "But other than needing a haircut and a razor, you don't look too bad. I even like the casual clothes better. You were almost too pretty in those expensive suits you wore."

Well, fuck. Again, she's thrown me for a loop. *Too pretty?* I can honestly say no one's ever accused me of that. Refusing to let her see that she's rattled me, my eyes drift over her. I don't bother being subtle about it because she certainly wasn't coy. "Well, it seems you have me all figured out. So why don't you tell me why you've flown your ivory tower and are here hiding away as well. Because trust me, princess, I've seen that same vacant look staring back at me for months now." I see her grimace at my use of *princess* and know she doesn't particularly like it. However, I learned long ago that it's easier to use a nickname than to possibly call a woman by the wrong name. And princess seems to suit her aloof manner.

She runs a fingertip around the rim of her recently replenished glass as she ponders my words. "We're all running from something, aren't we?" She dips a finger into her drink and sucks the alcohol from it. "I don't want to think about the reasons why I'm here, and I don't believe you do either."

Intrigued despite myself, I ask, "So what does that leave us to talk about, princess?"

Giving me a direct look that I recognize, she says, "At this point in my life, conversation is overrated. I'm sure we could make better use of your talents. I've heard you're very good at what you do."

I'm far from inexperienced, but I feel the need to clarify that she's indeed talking about what I think she is. What little I do know of her has never led me to believe she's the one-night-stand type, but unless I'm mistaken, she just propositioned me. "Are you saying you want me to fuck you?" Blunt and to the point—why bother with anything else?

Thankfully, she stops sucking the scotch off her finger and downs the glass before answering. "Yeah, I'm glad you picked up on that. Your place or mine?" She gets to her feet while I'm still trying to figure out what in the hell is going on. She takes a few steps and then stops when she sees I'm not following her. Looking confused, she asks, "What're you waiting for?"

I get to my feet and pull my wallet from my pocket. I toss some bills onto the table and slowly follow her. *What in the fuck is happening here?* The odd thing is that I'm not sure why I'm even questioning it. I've lost count of the number of women I've spent a few hours with in the last year. It's not complicated—it never is. It's certainly not a matter of me *not* finding her attractive, because she's gorgeous. Maybe it's her strong resemblance to Lia. Hell, that's not it. I doubt many men out there would refuse the chance to fuck the clone of their best friend's hot wife if given the opportunity. Women don't call us pigs for nothing. Shaking my head, I catch up with her at the parking lot. "Sorry, princess, you're not going to find your carriage here. I walked."

If I think that's going to deter her, I'm mistaken. "So did I. Which way to your place? I haven't done much housekeeping lately, and frankly, I'd like some clean sheets for a change."

This is turning into one of the most interesting nights I've had in a long time, so I just go with it. Tossing an arm over her shoulders, I point her in the direction of my house and nudge her forward. "What makes you think I have clean sheets or that you'll even make it to my bed?"

I expect her to toss some kind of insult at me. But without missing a beat, she says, "I figure I'll suck your dick against the wall as soon as we get there. Then we'll move on to the bedroom. You'll eat my pussy while you recover and then you'll fuck me. Probably from behind because I think you're an ass man."

Holy shit! Kara Jacks is a full-on, dirty-talking badass, and I'm going to fuck her so hard she'll still be feeling it next week. Even though I'm doing nothing but thinking of my cock in her mouth, I still manage to keep my voice level as I say, "Sounds like you've got it all figured out. You do this kind of thing every night?" I have no clue why that thought bothers me, but it does. I don't want to be just one in a long line of men she's fucked while she's here. This whole thing is messing with my head, so I do what I'm good at—I shut it down. Fucking doesn't require thinking. For most men, it's as natural as breathing and can be done on autopilot if needed.

"Do you really care?" she tosses back at me, and my silence hopefully gives her the answer. I apply slight pressure to her shoulders, steering her across the sand to the front door of the house I'm renting. I release her while I pull out the key and open the door. She steps into the dark foyer and stops, obviously waiting for me to flip the light on. Screw that. There's plenty of time later to see how she looks when she comes. Right now, I'm ready to ensure her words come to life.

With no further preamble, I close the door behind me and unbutton my shorts. The sound of my zipper lowering is like a gunshot in the room. I move until the wall is to my back and then issue my challenge. "Bring that mouth over here, princess, and show me what you've got." I grin as I hear a snort before her hand falls on my chest.

"You're nothing if not predictable," she says, and I can almost see her rolling her eyes at me. Her hand begins sliding lower, and my cock twitches as she palms it through my boxer briefs before pushing them down below my hips and releasing my dick. She wraps a hand around the heavy weight, effectively halting its mad bobbing.

My voice sounds a little strained, but I can't resist teasing her a bit more. "Don't make me the bad guy here.

You were the one begging to suck my cock. I'm just giving you what you want." She tightens her grip around my dick, and I grit my teeth, trying not to explode. So few women understand that men like a firm hand. Hell, even a little pain. Grab on and show it who's in charge.

Kara suddenly leans down, and fuck almighty—she goes for it. Her mouth has replaced her hand, and she completely skips the getting to know you phase and goes right to the main event. So many sensations come at me that I can barely process them. Her teeth are scraping against the sensitive skin at the underside of my dick; her tongue flicks the slit as if lapping cream from a bowl, and her hand holds the base in something like a chokehold. I'm sweating bullets and damn near close to crying for my fucking mommy when she moves on. I manage to draw a breath before she sucks me deep into her mouth and swallows around me. *Fuck!* I can't hold back. The contractions send me over the edge, and before I can stop myself, I'm shooting ribbons of cream down her throat. Normally, I'd at least give a woman fair warning before doing that, but hell, there simply wasn't time. She takes it all like a freaking porn star and then releases me with a pop. "I'm gonna admit, I saw that lasting longer." She laughs.

I should be offended at her jab of my control, but fuck it, she's right. Normally, that would have gone on for a while. I don't come until I want to. But I've never been with a woman who can suck cock like her. Add in the fact she's not just some random piece of ass, and there you have it, folks—fastest blowjob since my teen years. I couldn't give a shit, though. I'm not going to complain when I've just had the most explosive head of my life. "You've got a mouth on you, princess, I'll give you that," I admit wryly. I pull my briefs up and kick the shorts that have settled around my ankles to the side. I take her by the arm and navigate the darkness until I reach the lamp in the foyer. I flip the switch, and we both blink for a moment. Instead of leading the way to the bedroom, I push her ahead of me.

"Door at the end of the hall." We both know I just want to stare at her ass. Hell, screw just staring. My hand takes flight, and I deliver a solid smack, loving the way it feels against my palm. Nothing small in that area. It's firm but still womanly soft. She's right, I am an ass man, and fucking her from behind is definitely on the agenda for tonight.

"Nice," she tosses over her shoulder sarcastically but continues to walk. The bedroom is dark when we reach it, and I'm sliding my hand along the wall looking for the light switch when she halts me. "No, leave it off. I don't want you staring at me and turning this into some weird sex with my cousin encounter."

I throw my head back, laughing in surprise. "Luc is my best friend. I've never thought about making it with his wife." Her snort fills the room, and yeah, I like her just a little more. Call me an asshole, but other than Cassie, I'm used to women throwing themselves at me. There's never any talking back in the bedroom. If I spank them, they beg for more. There's little challenge in a woman you can do no wrong with. I have no doubt that Kara would call me on anything she didn't like. My manly pride and ego mean less than nothing to her. She's direct and to the point, so I'll be the same. "Take your clothes off and get on the bed. Lie on your back and spread your legs. We've reached the pussy eating part of the evening."

"Oh, goody," she deadpans. The rustling of her clothing lets me know she's following my directions. Then I hear the sound of the mattress depressing, and I quickly remove the rest of my clothing before finding my way to the bedside table. This shit would be a lot easier if I could actually see, but I'll respect her wishes . . . for now. I manage to locate a strip of condoms in the drawer and toss them on the bed. "Hey!" she snaps. "Could you not blind me with your gross of latex?"

I laugh once again. This chick seriously needs her ass slapped, and I'll be more than happy to take care of it.

"You wanted the dark, princess," I remind her. Any sarcastic quip she has is lost as I toss her legs over my shoulders and take my first lick. I'm certain I've died and gone to pussy heaven because she tastes like a ripe peach. Her legs wrap around me so tightly, I wonder if I'll die with my face buried in her wet heat, but I manage to wedge away far enough to draw a breath. Despite her tough demeanor, she's moaning like a whore in heat as I show no mercy. My tongue, my mouth, and my fingers are everywhere. She comes three times before I finally release her now limp body. I pat her leg, enjoying the sound of her heavy breathing as it fills the room. "Where's my sarcastic girl at now?" She surprises me by giggling, which goes straight to my cock. "Crawl up on the bed and get on your hands and knees. That ass is mine now."

My hand falls away as she shifts higher up on the mattress. "Just remember," she tosses out, "you haven't been cleared for the second slot, so please go directly to the first one."

Luckily, my eyes have adjusted to the darkness, and I can see her outline clearly. I put a knee on the bed and move up behind her. My hand settles on one firm ass cheek, and I rub it for a second before delivering a sharp smack. She grunts but doesn't voice an objection. *Good girl.* "I'm surprised you care, princess," I murmur as I continue to alternate stroking with spanking. "You certainly haven't been shy so far. Don't tell me that no man has ever fucked this ass. I find that very hard to believe."

"If you're stalling because you need more recovery time, just go ahead and admit it," she taunts. "You're getting a little age on you, so it's completely understandable you wouldn't be able to er . . . bounce back as fast as you could in your twenties."

She did not go there. Insult anything but my cock. I knew I should have insisted on keeping the lights on. Then she would have been aware I've yet to go soft. As phenomenal as her blowjob was, my dick stayed hard even after damn near choking her with my cum. Before she can toss out another dig at my manhood, I feel around, find the condoms, and quickly roll one on. I rub the tip of my cock through her wetness and grin as I hear her whimper. I grip her hips on either side and bury myself balls deep in her wet heat. And no surprise, she's a screamer. I find myself fucking her deeper and harder to see how vocal she can be, and she certainly doesn't disappoint. My ears are ringing, and I'm afraid the windows will shatter, but I fucking love it. She's ramming her hips back to meet mine, and we're going at it like animals. I'm determined to wring her dry before I come. I won't give the minx a reason to question my stamina. She'd enjoy that too much. "Take it, princess," I grunt as I slap her ass. I'm damn tempted to bury my finger there, but I'll let it go—this time.

"OH MY GOD," she yells loudly enough to wake the dead. "I'm—I'm . . . coming!" As her pussy clamps down even tighter and begins to contract around me, I speed up. I'm holding her in place; otherwise, she'd be across the bed as I give her everything I have. Even without her screeching it out, I count two more orgasms before I finally allow myself to be carried over the edge. I come so hard, dark spots dance in my vision. I just manage to pull out before we both collapse sideways in a tangled, sweaty heap. "You've got game, I'll give you that," she wheezes out.

I'm strangely pleased by her compliment. I mean it's not as if I had any doubts, but after her earlier sarcasm, it's nice to hear her actually admit I've impressed her. I have a feeling she doesn't toss many compliments around where men are concerned. Actually, I'm thinking more and more that she's the female version of me, which is either downright scary or hot as hell. I'm still trying to decide which. I give her ass a squeeze. "It's okay to admit I'm the best you've ever had, princess. We both know it's true."

She jabs me in the side with what feels like a surprisingly bony finger. "You're so damn cocky." After releasing a loud yawn, she mumbles, "Now, if you'll get off me, I need to find my clothes and head home. You've worn me out, Ace."

And here is where things get weird. "You can crash here for the rest of the night. No need to leave." *What the hell?* I have no idea why I keep blurting this shit out, even as my inner voice is screaming at me to shut up.

Apparently, I've shocked her as well, because the room is quiet for several long moments before she releases a long-suffering sigh. "All right, I'm too tired to argue. I'll stay since you've put yourself out there and I don't want to hurt your feelings, but we're not making a habit of this or anything, so don't be getting any ideas." She shimmies away from me in the darkness and crawls to the top of the bed. Within seconds, she's under the covers, and I'm still sitting at the bottom of the bed wondering what happened.

I get to my feet and dispose of the condom in the bathroom before brushing my teeth. I walk back into the bedroom and stand uncertainly. I'm actually tempted to go use one of the spare bedrooms, but I know without a doubt she'll call me a pussy if I do. I issued the invitation, and I need to man up and honor it. No big deal. I have spent the entire night with a woman before—just not often. Plus, Kara's kind of like extended family, right? Okay, maybe that wasn't a good analogy. You don't usually fuck your family. I release a breath and stalk to the other side of the bed and gingerly climb in. I'm practically hovering on the edge. One mistake and I'll be on the floor. Surprisingly enough, I'm tired and am on the verge of drifting off almost immediately. When the sound of a snore fills the room, I shake my head and smile. Of all the women in the world I could invite to sleep over, I pick the one who snores like a lumberjack.

CHAPTER TWO

Kara

I'm disoriented when I wake, which isn't exactly anything new for me. I've always been a heavy sleeper, and the medication I've taken on and off for the last year makes that worse. Still . . . the feeling of warmth at my back and the heavy weight across my side are certainly new as is the hand holding my breast. Based on the light in the room, I know the sun has been up for a while. I'd guess it's close to ten in the morning. Of course, that isn't really the big issue here. I appear to be completely naked, and I have what feels like a hard dick sticking between the crack of my ass. Those two things are a bit more urgent than the placement of the sun.

I turn my head slowly and release the breath I've been holding. Memories of the night before flood back, and I take a moment to stare at the man behind me while he's sleeping. He's a cocky and conceited ass, but there's no denying it: Aidan Spencer is drop-dead gorgeous. I feel myself getting wet from just looking at him. He's tall, dark, and delicious with a body that makes a woman want to throw her pride away and beg him for whatever scraps he'll give. And last night, he brought his A-game. I might have teased him, but truthfully, he fucked me stupid. I've never had it like that before. I was coming before he'd even fully penetrated me with that big cock of his. Heck, one flick of my clit right now and I'd go off just thinking about it. I wanted him again, and I hadn't allowed myself to double-dip in so very long. It's easier in my situation not to form attachments.

I'd been shocked to see him last night. I haven't been feeling particularly social lately, so I'd only been to the outdoor bar a few times. I'd been at a loose end and didn't feel like another night of staring at the walls. And truthfully, I'd been looking for a distraction. I've been staying at Uncle Lee's for a few weeks, and the solitude I thought I wanted has already become too much. My parents were suffocating me with their concern at home, but I'm no happier here. Truthfully, I have no idea what to do next. I have my business degree, and I've always planned to work full time for Uncle Lee. I've interned at Falco Industries during summer vacations for years before my world was suddenly tipped on its side.

When you're twenty-two, you think you're invincible. I was in my last semester of college, and the only stress in my life at that point was passing my finals. The day my doctor called me and used words like malignant, treatments, and appointments, my blissful world fell apart. *I fell apart.* I'd thanked her and called my dad, delivering the news that following a routine yearly physical, a lump had been found in my breast. The biopsy revealed malignant cancer. My world became a very dark place. That began months of anxiety, depression, and a whole lot of denial. I'd wanted to bury my head in the sand and act like nothing was wrong. Luckily, with my parents, that wasn't an option. My father had taken charge, and the next morning, we were sitting in the office of the best oncologist in North Carolina. I had Stage 2 breast cancer, which meant the tumor was growing but only found in the breast. Even though I was given the option of a lumpectomy, I chose a mastectomy instead. My father agreed it was a better choice, and I wasn't really in the state of mind to do the research myself. As a safety precaution, I had radiation five days a week for seven weeks.

Apparently, radiation has fewer side effects than chemotherapy, so I was lucky. *REALLY?* Somehow, I didn't feel like a lottery winner when I was hugging my toilet and throwing up what little I'd managed to choke down due to the difficulty of swallowing. And the horrible tightness in my chest that never seemed to go away. I would have panic attacks and feel as if I couldn't draw enough air into my lungs. My doctor said that many of my side effects were a result of the anxiety I was suffering. He put me on antidepressants, which made me into little more than a zombie. It did help with the tightness in my chest, though, and lessened my nausea. The downside? I wanted to do nothing but sleep.

After I finished my treatments, I had reconstruction surgery. After my breast was removed, I could hardly stand to look at myself in the mirror. The puckered scars reminded me every day of what I'd lost. It was impossible to forget I'd had cancer when the empty bra cup reminded me constantly. I had expected a huge wave of relief to fill me with my reconstructed breast, so I resented its foreign feel. It was almost as if I blamed *it* for everything, which was absurd. No one ever said that anything about having cancer was rational. Eventually, I learned to accept it but continued to mourn the loss of the one cut from my body. The scars were minimal thanks to a skilled surgeon, but I could see them because I knew where to look. Anyone else would have to study that breast closely to see the thin silvery lines.

It's been almost a year since I finished my last round of radiation, yet I haven't been able to get off the anti-depressants. Even now, when I'm officially in remission and cancer-free, I'm terrified that the anxiety and depression will return should I go off them. Before my cancer, I felt invincible with my whole life ahead of me.

Now, I know it can all be taken away in the blink of an eye. Cancer took many things from me, but probably the most shattering was my innocence and the belief that nothing bad could ever happen to me. Even with my medication, I find myself constantly looking ahead and checking for any sign of trouble. A simple case of the sniffles is enough to send me into full-blown panic mode. I will never again assume that a minor illness is nothing. I'll always be waiting for the other shoe to drop. Or in this case, for the cancer to return. I'm no longer Kara Jacks, daughter of Peter and Charlotte Jacks. Nor am I simply sister to Kyle Jacks. No, first and foremost, at least in my mind, I'm Kara Jacks, cancer *survivor*.

It's insane the things that went through my head after I completed radiation. I mourned the fact that I could never fill out a health history form without checking the box for cancer. Then having to use the space provided below to explain. Before my diagnosis, I'd loved my ample C-cups. Afterward, I found myself wondering if I was being punished for my vanity in displaying them in low-cut tops. As if dressing more demurely would have kept me from getting cancer.

Again, the word lucky is something I hear far too often. *You're so lucky you caught it early. You're so lucky it hasn't spread. You're so lucky they got it all.* Then I feel like a fucking ungrateful bitch who doesn't deserve to be cancer-free because I don't feel lucky. Am I glad to be alive and in remission? Absolutely. But nowhere in there do I feel fortunate. Instead, I've let myself become the victim. Cancer took away my power, and I've yet to wrestle it back. That mindset is the reason I'm here now. I love my parents, but I can't regain my independence while they're standing over me wringing their hands every time I grimace. I'm feeding their paranoia and in turn, they're feeding mine. It's not their fault—far from it. I wouldn't have gotten through everything that I have without them firmly by my side. Now, it's time for me to put myself back together again. I need to find the confident, fearless woman I once was and bring her back again.

Amazingly enough, a version of that person made an appearance for the first time in a year last night, and it was almost effortless. I'm no virgin, and I'm no whore. I've had sex. I've been in casual relationships. I went through a spell after my cancer-free announcement where I felt the need to reaffirm that I was still alive and sex was the way I did it. But it was different with Aidan. Possibly because he's not just a face in a crowd. We're not friends, but we're connected through family. I shocked myself as I joked, taunted, flirted, and propositioned him. It was so easy. He wanted me, and he didn't bother to hide it. He didn't see me as broken and flawed. He spanked me, for God's sake. He was rough, but there were also moments of gentleness that I wouldn't have expected. I know it's insane, but he patched a part of me that's been broken. I'm not naïve enough to say it's fixed, but neither is it completely cracked open anymore.

For the first time in so long, I liked who I was and could tell he did as well. I don't think Aidan has been with many women who don't worship at his feet. I was fun and fearless with him. But how will that translate in the light of the day? Will I crawl back into my shell and retreat to my self-pity-filled existence thus losing what little ground I feel I've gained? The very thought fills me with dread and spurs me into action. I'm not ready to find out. I need to get out of here before he wakes up. I want him to remember the Kara from earlier and not the version I've allowed myself to become.

It's no easy feat, but I manage to slip out of his arms and slide to the edge of the bed. Even though my bladder feels as if it's going to burst, I don't risk using the bathroom. Instead, I quickly gather my clothes and tiptoe down the hallway. I dress in the foyer before quietly opening the door and stepping outside. The sun is high in the sky and temporarily blinds me as it reflects back from the ocean. I curse under my breath as I realize that my walk of shame is going to be long. I'm not about to go back inside and wake Aidan, though. My newfound confidence is fragile at best, and I plan to cling to it with everything I have. I can't see Aidan again until I know if last night was just a fluke or if I've possibly turned some type of corner. Because either I've finally gone crazy or Aidan Spencer fucked me back to life. Dear God, I can only imagine how big his already inflated ego will expand if he ever hears those words.

Aidan

I roll over in bed and rub a hand over my dry, gritty eyes. I'm normally up shortly after dawn to go for a run on the beach. This morning, I know it's much later as the room is fully awash in sunlight. Needing another five minutes before I rise, I turn onto my stomach and grab a pillow to tuck under my head. That's when it hits me. I bolt upright and look around the room. Her scent is all around me, but I know instinctively she's gone. The house has its usual vacant feeling.

I flop backward and think of the previous night. My cock hardens and the sheet tents as I remember driving into her tight, wet pussy. If she were here now, she'd be riding me while I fucked her into oblivion, but she's not. *So this is how it feels to be a one-night stand.* Kara seems determined to give me more firsts in twenty-four hours than I've had in years. She picked me up, tossed out all kinds of veiled insults about my sexual prowess, and now, she's taken off without a word. *Fuck, man up, Spencer.* Am I actually lying here wallowing in pity because she didn't say goodbye? I should be relieved. A sleepover was weird enough, but did I actually want her to hang around the next morning? Maybe have breakfast and spend the day together? *Hell no!* She saved us both some awkwardness. Granted, I wouldn't be averse to her handling this near painful case of morning wood, but isn't that a big reason God gave us hands? I toss the pillow containing her scent onto the floor and get up. I make quick work of stripping the sheets and tossing them in the corner with the pillow. I'll wash them later so I'm not reminded of her tonight.

Even though I call myself all kinds of pussy, I still walk through the house to confirm she is indeed gone, and I try my best to ignore the feeling of disappointment. Shit, maybe it is time to go home. I'm obviously more in need of human contact than I thought. Maybe I'll email Luc later on to check in. We haven't been apart this long since we met and it's doing a number on me. I miss my best friend, and I'm beginning to realize that I'm reaching the point where I need the people I love to complete the healing process.

I shrug off my melancholy and go about my usual morning routine—just a little later than usual. By the time I've run five miles, showered, and had lunch, I'm feeling much more like myself. If not for her lingering fragrance, I could almost pretend Kara Jacks never crashed into my world the previous night. *Almost.*

CHAPTER THREE

Kara

What are you doing? Leave now before he sees you. My subconscious continues to beg and plead for me to see reason as I approach Aidan's house. It's already after seven in the evening so he likely isn't even at home. I'll knock once, and if he doesn't answer, I'll leave. I glance down and cringe at the bag I'm carrying. I stopped by the store on my way and bought a bottle of wine, a couple of steaks, and a bag of potatoes. Not only am I showing up unannounced, but I'm bringing dinner as well. How pathetically hopeful. This would give him enough material to crack jokes at my expense for days. That is, if he doesn't just flat out tell me to go away.

And dammit, I'm dressed in skimpy shorts and a tank top. I might as well be holding a sign that says, "Please fuck me again, you stud." It's not as if he came looking for me today. Obviously, he had no intentions of an encore performance. Even knowing all of this, I still raise my hand and rap it against the wooden door. My heart is beating frantically in my chest, and I feel just a tad lightheaded. *Shit, what is wrong with me?*

I've almost convinced myself to flee while I can when the door opens, and Aidan stands before me looking more than a little surprised. He recovers quickly, and his lips quirk in amusement as he settles against the doorframe. "Well, hello, princess. To what do I owe this honor?" Before I can answer, the ass actually wiggles his brows and smirks at me. "Couldn't stay away from my big dick, could you?" He steps out of the doorway and tosses an arm over my shoulders before lowering his voice. "It's understandable so no need to be embarrassed. You obviously haven't had a good fuck in years and last night rocked your world." My mouth is flapping open and closed as I sputter for a scalding reply. He points at the bag dangling limply from my fingers. "Whatcha got in there? Some lube so we can visit the ole forbidden door tonight?"

Thank God I snap out of my daze and poke him in the side with my elbow. "You're so damn full of yourself, aren't you?"

He throws his head back and laughs. "I hate to point this out, princess, but you're the one who came to me. And considering you begged for my cock mere hours ago, I can only assume you're back for more."

Why does he keep calling me princess? Probably so he won't fuck up and call me by the wrong name. Typical ass. I narrow my eyes as I glare at him. Then apparently, I lose my mind right along with him because I begin giggling. He's so outrageous that it's impossible to remain immune to his crude humor. "You're so full of crap, Spencer," I say as I shrug off his arm and walk into the house. I hear his footsteps behind me, but I continue a bit farther until I'm forced to ask, "Where's the kitchen?" He actually puts a hand on my ass and guides me down the hallway and into a modern kitchen that would no doubt be a chef's dream. There's stainless steel and granite galore. In addition, a wall of windows provides a breathtaking view of the ocean. Uncle Lee's house is amazing, but this one has warmth. "Not bad," I admit before setting my bag on the counter. I pull the steaks out and wave them in front of his face. "Do you know how to use a grill or am I going to be forced to do everything?"

He gives me a lazy grin, letting me know I've walked right into some type of verbal trap. "I've got the meat covered, princess. I'll make it so good for you that you'll be begging me for it."

Shaking my head, I smile despite myself. "You're such a pig. I can't imagine why you're home by yourself tonight. I'm sure somewhere out there is a dim-witted woman who would love to spend the evening with you. You might have to keep the insults simple—you know, nothing over four letters. Of course, that's pretty much your limit as well, isn't it?" I'm busy looking through the drawers for a wine cork so I don't see him move until he's wrapped his arms around me from behind and pulled me against his chest.

"Shhh," he whispers into my hair. "There's no need for all that jealousy, baby. I'll tie you to my bed tonight and fuck you so good you'll be purring like the pretty little pussy I know you are in no time. Now, put those claws away and just enjoy the moment."

"God, you're insufferable," I grumble but don't move away as he kisses his way down my neck. I feel him harden against my ass, and I'm ready to toss dinner aside and get to the entertainment portion of the evening. I have no idea what this man has done to me, but he seems to have a direct line to my clit. I'm wet and ready just from a little light petting, which is completely out of character for me. As if he knows what I'm thinking, one hand moves around to my front and wedges its way into the top of my skintight shorts. He groans when his fingers slip easily through my sex.

"Looks like someone needs some attention," he murmurs as he begins to stroke my traitorous flesh. I moan. Why can't I resist him? I've been with men who actually brought me flowers and begged to see me again. Yet I choose to chase this one? His ego is so big; I'm surprised anything else can fit in the house with it. Still, my panties are wet, and I'm panting like I've just run a marathon. All from a little dirty talk and his hand. When one of his thick fingers slides inside me—that's it, I'm coming and moaning as if I've just had the best sexual experience of my life. He chuckles as he wrings every last drop of pleasure from me before calmly removing his hand. I'm almost certain he's licking his fingers, but I'm still too frazzled to turn around and see. Then he throws my words from the previous night back at me. "I'm gonna admit, princess, I saw that lasting longer." *What a dickhead!*

I push away from him. "Obviously, we both have control problems. I'll work on mine if you do the same."

"Nicely done," he replies, not sounding offended in the least. It takes a very secure man to handle insults to his masculinity, and Aidan is certainly that. From my experience, he doesn't have an equal between the sheets, and I'm quite certain he knows it.

We work in harmony as he prepares the steaks and I handle the potatoes. We decide to eat outside on the deck since the weather is fairly mild. Then almost as if we've done it for years instead of just a night, we end up in the bedroom and true to his earlier threat, using two T-shirts, he ties my hands to the headboard. I give him points for improvising to which he proudly informs me that he was a Boy Scout. He goes on to prove to me in great detail just how he earned his merit badges. I'm betting the troop leader would be horrified, but I say it gives new meaning to their logo, "*Prepared for life.*"

Aidan

Once again, I'm lying in the dark with Kara curled in my arms. It wouldn't be a lie to say tonight was one of the best evenings I've ever had with a woman. We joked around, picking on each other as we ate dinner and drank a bottle of wine. Then we walked on the beach before the sight of her in those tiny shorts made me so hard I practically dragged her inside, tied her up, and fucked her with everything I had. We grabbed a quick shower afterward, and without saying a word, she'd dropped her towel and crawled into the bed. Thankfully, her back was to me, and she didn't see me standing uncertainly before finally getting in behind her. This time, she'd turned over and tossed an arm across my waist and her leg over the top of mine. I'll admit that for a few moments, I was close to panic. I'm not one to cuddle. I don't even know how really. I mean, I don't immediately toss a woman from the bed and show her the door. Normally, I go straight for the shower, which gets them up and on their way afterward. They go home clean and happy, and I go to sleep—alone. Works well for everyone. Until Kara. She's like the guest who came to dinner then never left. However, strangely enough, despite my moment of panic, I'm glad she's here.

Being with her is easy. Hell, I don't believe the shit that comes out of her mouth. She's such a hard-ass. I love getting a rise out of her, and she never disappoints. At the same time, I feel guilty. I've stopped my brooding for a few days and have enjoyed myself with a woman. No matter how intimate it may seem, fucking can actually be very impersonal, even when you're going down on a woman. I take care of her first and make sure she comes a respectable number of times before I find my own release. I've spent years perfecting my art, and I'm certain no woman has been left unsatisfied. It's almost turned into something like orgasm production. I turn out an exceptional product and then send it on down the line. Yeah, I'm aware it makes me sound like a complete asshole, but as long as everyone gets what they need, is there truly a problem?

This friendship or whatever this is with Kara is different for me. I haven't fallen instantly in love with her or anything, but it's disturbing that Cassie has barely entered my mind since meeting Kara last night. In fact, most of those waking hours have been centered on fucking, sleeping with, or thinking of Kara. I guess maybe I should look at it in a positive way. It could be an indication that I'm ready to move on. Before Cassie died, I briefly considered if I was in love with the dream girl I considered her more than anything else. She, Lucian, and I were best friends for many years, and maybe that long-term friendship clouded my judgment. I blame myself for not being able to save her, but how long can that continue? I walked away from my whole life for damn near a year trying to resolve my feelings into something more manageable. Drinking copious amounts of alcohol and fucking every female who walked. On repeat. Alcohol helped to numb the pain, and the women filled some of those vulnerable night hours when I think too much.

A part of me wants to pack my stuff tomorrow and just drive. Leave this confusing whatever it is with Kara behind and decide if I'm ready to go home and return to my life. But even as I think that, she mutters something in her sleep and burrows closer to me. It's insane because I can't help but feel that I'm as much of a lifeline to her right now as she is becoming to me. I know very little about her other than she's Lia's cousin. I have no idea if she takes up with virtual strangers regularly or if she's on the rebound from a bad relationship. Or could it be that she's fucked up over something and trying to escape as well? I'm curious enough that I'm tempted to email Luc and ask about her, but I don't feel comfortable invading her privacy in that way. Plus, like me, she may be here to escape from something and wouldn't want everyone knowing where to find her. Although, she is using her uncle's house so he at least knows.

I've lain awake in this bed every night for months trying to purge myself of the sorrow and guilt I feel over Cassie's death. But with Kara here, I am almost at peace for the first time in so fucking long. I realize she's not some kind of magic pill to cure my problems, but not feeling as if acid is eating away at my very soul is more of a relief than I could have imagined. I hadn't realized how torturous the long nights were until I *wasn't* staring at the clock and watching the minutes tick by so slowly. If she needs an escape as badly as I do and we can give that to each other, then why not? We're consenting adults who have made no promises to each other. With my track record, I can't say I won't be ready to see the last of her tomorrow. But for now, she's helping me burn through the hours, and I'm too selfish to let that go. It would be preferable if she didn't have ties with Luc and Lia, but maybe that's what draws me to her so much. She's a piece of home after being adrift. If Luc kicks my ass at some point in the future, then hopefully it will have been worth it. Fuck, who am I kidding? The first night alone was worth it.

A quick glance at the bedside table shows an hour has passed, which I consider nothing short of a miracle. Even when she's asleep, Kara still manages to occupy my mind easily. So I allow myself to relax and put my hand over hers where it rests on my stomach. Nothing is happening here but companionship. It could be that I've been wrong to avoid that in my life because this feels pretty damn good. Surrounded by her scent, I'm lulled to sleep with nothing more on my mind than what tomorrow will bring—with her.

CHAPTER FOUR

Kara

My daily routine of going to Aidan's in the evening has become familiar and addictive. It's been two weeks since we met in that bar and I've spent every night since in his bed. After the first week, he started leaving the door either unlocked or hanging open, so I took that to mean I didn't need to knock. Sometimes, we went out for dinner, but most of the time, we cooked together.

I had the uneasy feeling I was replacing my parents with him. People with anxiety or depression tend to have what is called a "safe person." Basically, it's someone who makes you feel more secure and less anxious when you're around them. The whole point of this time away was to regain my independence, but am I really doing that? Sure, I'm happier and more relaxed than I've been in months. I could literally go hours without thinking about cancer, which is a big step in the right direction. What happens when this is over? Eventually, both of us will return home and probably not together. He isn't whispering words of love and long-term plans in my ear each night as he fucks me senseless. This is commonly referred to as a summer fling. What will become of me at the end of it if I'm indeed transferring my dependence onto him?

I am still mulling that disturbing question over in my mind when I arrive at his door to find a note stuck to it. *On the beach. Come on down, beautiful.* And there it is, something I never expected to feel for him: a big case of the warm fuzzies. He doesn't owe me anything. I'm not his girlfriend, and we never made official plans. But he lets me know where he is and asks me to join him. Therefore, I walk around the front and look around the mostly deserted beach until I finally spot him striding out of the ocean— with a woman. She is blonde and scantily clad in a swimsuit that is no more than tiny scraps of cloth held together by equally small strings. I instantly hate her. I stalk across the warm sand before realizing I'm jealous and doing nothing to hide it. Thankfully, Aidan has yet to notice me so I take a moment to regroup. I need to get it together. I can't let him see that the other woman bothers me. We are both free to see other people. I may want to order the bimbo to take a hike, but I have no rights at all where he is concerned. *Is he testing me?* He'll probably be amused by such a display from me, and dammit, I'm not going to give him the pleasure of watching me have a tantrum over him. So I plaster on a bright smile—that I am far from feeling—and proceed forward. When I'm a few feet away, he looks away from beach Barbie and spots me.

"There you are." He grins lazily when I reach them. The eager woman next to him is now clutching his elbow as if terrified he's going to get away. "Kara, this is my neighbor, Brandy. She was offering to give me some surf lessons."

Oh, I'll just bet she was. Women can usually read each other, and I know with absolute certainty that it wasn't a board Brandy wanted him to ride. "That sounds like fun," I say in a bored tone. Brandy gives me a fake smile full of teeth. Actually, it's more like a snarl. "I wouldn't mind learning how myself."

I fight the urge to laugh as Brandy's lips pinch together tightly. "I only have two boards," she says in a voice dripping with false regret. Before I can reply, she does a quick subject change. "So, Aidan, how about that drink tonight?" She trails a finger up his biceps before adding, "I really enjoyed our last time together."

Instead of looking uncomfortable, Aidan appears amused. "Kara and I already have plans this evening, but maybe I'll catch you later in the week." Brandy is ecstatic with that half promise, assuring him that she is just a phone call away. I focus all my energy on keeping my face impassive even though I want nothing more than to knee him in the balls. The bastard didn't bat an eye when he promised a date with another woman right in front of me. Maybe we aren't a couple, but he could have a little class. He's fucked me every night for two weeks. Doesn't that entitle me to a small offering of courtesy? *Obviously not to this asshole. I'm done with that.*

As Brandy rushes off with half her ass hanging out each side of her swimsuit, I turn away and begin marching back in the direction I came. I didn't give a shit at this point if I looked jealous or not. "Go away," I mutter as he easily catches up to me.

"You're pissed," he states sounding curious.

"Wow, way to state the obvious," I snap. I am no match for his long strides, so getting away from him is impossible, which makes me even angrier. He halts in his tracks as I whirl around. "Why don't you go back and take Brandy up on her offer? Apparently, it wouldn't be the first time."

"Green looks good on you, princess," he murmurs. "You hate the thought that I've fucked her, don't you?"

"Screw you!" I hiss as I turn away. His hand clamps around my arm preventing me from running. *Great.* Not only am I humiliating myself, but he is also forcing me to stay and endure it.

Looking serious for the first time, he says, "She was nothing more than a past distraction and not even that good of one. I tossed her a bone because she's become a nuisance and I wanted to get rid of her." He uses his leverage to pull me against his chest, closing his arms around my stiff body. His mouth lowers to my ear as he whispers, "Why would I have any desire to fuck her when I have you?"

I push against his hold, trying to resist. "You don't have me," I argue weakly as his lips slide over the sensitive skin of my neck. "I'm going home, and I'm not coming back."

"Bullshit," he purrs as he lowers a hand to my ass, pressing me firmly against the hard swell of his arousal. "We may not know what the hell we're doing otherwise, but in that bed every night, we both get everything we need."

I make one last attempt to salvage my pride. "Fuck you." But it sounds like a token protest, even to my ears.

"Oh, that's exactly what I'm going to do very soon, baby," he promises as he thrusts against me. "We're going inside, and I'm going to bend you over the table and bury my cock inside you." In a whirl of motion, we are through the door of his house, and he is shoving my shorts down my legs while I toss my shirt and bra off. His swim trunks hit the floor next, and somehow, a condom magically appears in his hand. I hook my fingers in the sides of my thong, ready to remove it when he puts a hand out to stop me. "Leave it." I am busy trying to figure out what he has planned with my underwear in place when he flips the thin lacy material aside and nudges his cock against my entrance. *Holy hotness.* I would have never imagined that being fucked while still wearing my panties would be hotter than being completely nude, but it feels so naughty. "Hold on to the edges of the table," he orders, and I have just curled my fingers around the wooden surface when he buries his big dick to the hilt inside me.

"Ah! Aidan!" I yell as my core immediately begins contracting around his girth.

"Not yet, princess," he growls as he smacks my ass. "That orgasm is mine. You don't come until I give you permission."

What the hell? I don't take orders from him. I'll come when I'm damn well ready. But then a funny thing happens. It's as if my pussy has given Aidan control. The brink that I'd been hovering on seems to get further and further away. "Damn you," I hiss in frustration as my body clamors for a release that won't come. He is pounding me hard, pulling almost all the way out and slamming back inside. His arms reach around me and palm my breasts, pinching my nipples. Little does he know that I feel nothing in one of them. He could lick, suck, and touch it all he wants, but I feel very little sensation there since my surgery. Just watching him touch the new breast is almost enough to derail the hum of desire flowing through my body. I want to jerk his hand away and tell him not to bother wasting his time, but it obviously excites him, and I certainly don't want to say anything that would require an explanation on my part. Aidan has no idea I'm partially broken, and I want it to remain that way. So I shut my eyes and focus on his dick sliding in and out of me. Within moments, I'm strung tight and trembling with my need for release. "Aidan, please," I pant, needing him to do something NOW.

He slams inside me twice more before shouting, "Come now!" And that's it. Wave after wave of pleasure grips my body as I spasm around him. His cock jerks and I know he's hit his own peak as well. He slows his pace but continues to move in me for another minute before pulling out. I collapse limply against the table, releasing the death grip that my hands have had on the corners. He lays a hand on my back. "You okay, princess?"

"All good," I wheeze as I attempt to slow my racing heart and catch my breath.

"Let's grab a quick shower and then walk down to the bar for a burger and a beer. I think I wore you out too much to cook."

I manage to pull myself up without wobbling, which is no easy feat. It takes me an embarrassingly long time to reach the bathroom, and by the time I get there, Aidan is already stepping out of the shower. The bastard gives me a knowing grin and drops a hard kiss on my lips before sauntering into the bedroom to dress. As always, his lips on mine rattle me. We've kissed while fucking, but we don't make a habit out of it. I think we both tend to avoid the intimacy of that particular act. I force myself to follow his example and make quick work of washing. I throw my damp hair into a ponytail and redress in the clothes that had been so hastily shed earlier.

Luckily, he didn't rip my panties off this time—as he so often does—so my undergarments are intact as we walk hand in hand to our favorite beach bar. I'll admit, I'd been taken aback the first time he reached for my hand. There are sides to him I haven't expected. For a man who keeps sex casual, he is surprisingly touchy-feely and has no problem with public displays of affection. At some point in one of our outings, he kissed me in full view of others as if it were the most natural thing in the world. After I'd gotten over the initial shock, I found I enjoyed it—maybe too much. It made me feel special, which I knew was a recipe for disaster. We weren't going to date, fall in love, get engaged, and then eventually marry. That isn't what this was. He lost the love of his life last year, and quite simply, I'd lost my way since cancer entered my life. Perhaps, he needed to learn how to live again just as badly as I did. I come back to the present with a start as Aidan nudges me to indicate that our server is waiting for my order. I hope my face gives no clues as to what I've been thinking about as I manage to say, "I'll have a glass of sangria please." Aidan orders a beer, and we're left alone once again.

Out of nowhere, he asks, "So what's up with the black hair now? You were a blonde like Lia, so that's a pretty drastic change."

I sense nothing negative in his question; he simply sounds curious. *But it has been two weeks. Two weeks and he is only just asking.* I shrug my shoulders, trying to look casual. "Just going through a phase." I take a sip of the sangria the server just put in front of me before adding, "I'm sure you'd rather be making it with a blonde, but you can't have everything you want, can you?" In truth, I'd colored my hair not long after I found out about my cancer. Maybe it was silly, but I needed to be in control of something and that was the easiest fix. My poor parents had been speechless when their normally golden-haired daughter had shown up looking more goth. To their credit, they'd even managed some feeble compliments on how the dark color made my green eyes stand out. I'm sure they hoped I'd change it back somewhere down the line, but a year later, I'm still sporting the dark color. I've thought of going back to my original shade, but right now, I'm not that person. And maybe it's foolish, but I feel as if I'd be living a lie to pretend that I'm who I was before cancer. *Two words. Before cancer.* That is how my life is now defined. Before . . . and after. Everyone else around me, bar my parents, of course, have seemingly kept cruising unaffected through their lives. *Why don't they know I feel like a shattered version of myself? Why can't they see I'm stuck?*

Aidan peels pieces of the label from his beer bottle, seeming fascinated by the task. "Other than you, I've had very little of what I want," he murmurs absently. I wonder if he's even aware of what he's admitted. Things between us are normally light and easy, so his admission seems rather deep.

I ponder giving a flippant remark to get us back on track, but fuck it. Why can't we be real with each other? They say there's freedom in talking to a shrink because of the whole neutral party thing. You don't know them, and they don't know you. In a way, Aidan and I have that type of association. We may have some vague connections, but there's no history between us, and whatever we've been doing will end when we leave the refuge of this beach town. We both have a temporary, non-judgmental sounding board. I have no one else in my life that I can admit to having bad days and that I'm struggling. The people who know of my cancer think I should be thrilled to be given the all clear. I feel as if I must maintain the happy façade around them. Like my *get out of cancer-free* card will be revoked if I don't appear grateful 24/7. I decide to test the waters by saying, "Yeah, I know the feeling. Life hasn't exactly been handing out all of my favorite things either. I guess that's why I'm hiding out here along with you."

He looks up, appearing almost startled at my words. "What's haunting you, princess?"

Dammit, what do I say? I clear my throat as I stall for time. I'm not sure what I expected when I decided on this sharing moment, because I do not intend to actually tell him the reason I'm so messed up. I opt at the last minute for a piece of the truth, hoping that'll be enough. "I've just had a stressful few years. I had a health scare, and I'm taking a little time away to recover."

Instead of looking satisfied, he appears hyper-alert. "You're sick?" His eyes run over me as if searching for something obvious.

I'm close to panicking when I have a moment of brilliance. "It was um . . . a female thing," I stammer convincingly. No man is brave enough to swim in those waters. No doubt, visions of heavy flow tampons and pads are going through his mind right now as he shifts uncomfortably in his seat. "I'm all right, but it kind of did a number on me. I needed some time away to you know . . . deal with it." I almost feel sorry for him; because it's obvious he doesn't know how to respond. Men are very basic when it comes to girl issues. They automatically think it relates to your period. He probably imagines I had one that lasted for months, which is even more terrifying for him. That would entail a prolonged period of PMS, which hell, isn't far off now that I think about it. I certainly had the mood swings and the misery.

"Yeah . . . er, that's—tough. I can see how you'd be in need of a break." He actually leans forward and pats my hand in almost a fatherly gesture. I resist the urge to giggle because it's pretty darn cute.

"Thanks," I choke out. "How are you doing? You've been away from home for a while now, haven't you? Any closer to what you're seeking?"

His face shutters. I'm not expecting an answer so I'm surprised when he says, "I'm not sure that you ever find rational answers to heavy shit. I've come to realize lately that it's more about peace or at the very least acceptance. I left because I didn't think it possible to find either of those things in a place full of memories and around people who meant well, but made it worse. There are times that only solitude will give you a reprieve from your problems."

I know he's talking about Cassie, but his struggles sound so similar to mine that I have to blink away the moisture that's gathered in the corners of my eyes. He doesn't need my sympathy any more than I need his. We've both had that in abundance from others, and it only breeds more depression. "How do you get your life back, though?" I ask, hoping he has more insight into that than I've found. When I look ahead, I see myself still in limbo ten years from now if I don't find the strength to stop being a victim.

He squeezes my hand so tightly that I wince, but bite my tongue to keep from breaking the moment we're in. Aidan is usually all jokes and lightness. This is an unguarded and raw moment of honesty from him and I'm riveted by it. *By him.* "I don't know, Kara. I wish I had that answer. For me, I'm trying to accept that I've spent roughly twenty years of my life loving an illusion. The sweet and innocent girl I grew up worshipping probably never existed. I put her on a pedestal complete with a crown and even though I witnessed her destructive personality so many times, I turned a blind eye to it."

"That's natural when you love someone," I say softly. "You only want to see the good in them."

He pinches the bridge of his nose with his other hand, suddenly looking so very tired. "I know, but I can't help but wonder if I'd actually acknowledged how deep her problems ran, would I have been able to get her the help she needed before she wreaked destruction on not only her life, but on Lucian and Lia's as well."

"Aidan, that's a big burden to put on yourself. There's no way you could have predicted that she'd try to kill Lia and then take her own life. And she did get help at some point, right? My father mentioned that she'd spent many years in a mental facility before the attack on Lia."

"Do you know what put her in that hospital?" he asks, and I shake my head.

"No, I never knew the reason."

He looks torn, as if not sure he wants to go any further. I want to urge him on as something tells me this is a big part of what torments him. But I also know how it feels when people pry into your private life so I wait silently. He turns slightly, motioning for Charlie, the bartender to bring him his usual scotch. When it arrives, he tosses it back and then holds up a finger for another, which he sets in front of him within easy reach. I think whatever he has to say must be really bad if he needs a backup of liquid courage. "I won't go through the whole history, but Cassie, Luc, and I were childhood friends. Cassie always loved Luc, and I was crazy about her. They dated in high school, and we all went to college together and shared an apartment. Cassie had been on medication for bi-polar disorder for years by this point. When she got pregnant, she had to go off the medication, and her mental health deteriorated rapidly. She was either riding a manic high or weeping from a depressed low. She and Luc were fighting almost non-stop. She was on him the minute he walked in every day with one accusation after another. It became so bad that even I couldn't stand to be around her. I stayed out as late as possible every night and left when I got up."

When he pauses to take a gulp from his glass, I say, "Wow, that had to be a very toxic environment for all of you. Why didn't you move out?" I couldn't imagine loving someone enough to stay in those circumstances, especially when the person was pregnant with another man's child.

He appears lost in thought as he says, "I wanted to, but I was afraid of what would happen. I knew Cassie was becoming increasingly erratic, and I was worried she would hurt herself." The hand still holding mine trembles and I reach out to cover it with my other one. "Anyway . . . I came home early one evening, which was unusual. I hadn't been in the mood to party and hoped that things would be quiet enough for me to have an early night. There was no sign of Luc or Cassie when I arrived, but Luc's car was there so I thought maybe they'd walked somewhere close by for a late dinner. As I was going down the hallway, I'd paused outside their room, and for a reason I'll never understand, I opened their door to check on them."

My eyes fly to his face as I hear the quiver in his voice. He's struggling with this part of the story, and I wish we weren't in such a public place so I could comfort him more. "You don't have to finish this here," I say, feeling as if I've pushed him into something that's tearing him apart, while I told him nothing about my actual problems.

He moves his chair closer to mine before saying, "I want you to know so you'll understand at least some of it." His leg is bouncing against mine under the table, a clear sign of his agitation. I'm so accustomed to the relaxed Aidan that this version is jarring. "So . . . when I opened the door, I didn't immediately know what had happened. That didn't come 'til later. All I saw was blood . . . so much of it that finding the source seemed impossible until I heard Luc choking and clutching his neck."

"Oh, dear God," I whisper in horror, but Aidan continues as if unaware of my interruption.

"Cassie had slashed Luc's neck, then both of her wrists." Taking a deep breath, he added, "Before stabbing herself in the abdomen." I can only gape at him in shock as he goes through what happened that night. What must it have done to this beautiful man beside me to find his two best friends like that? It's a testament to his strength that instead of falling apart as most anyone would have done, he held it together and saved their lives. Without him, there is no way they would have lived until the ambulance arrived. "Cassie had what they called a psychotic break after that. She had no awareness of people or surroundings for years until she was given a new, experimental drug. Then it was as if she came alive almost overnight. Luc was freaked out when her doctor did a trial run by letting her out for a weekend. He was completely against it, but I . . . God, she seemed like her old self, back before we all lived together. I took a leave of absence and rented a place near the hospital so she could spend weekends with me. Each time I saw her, she was better. We'd talk about fun times from our childhood, but she didn't say much about Luc or mention what she'd done to him. I reasoned she kept that blocked out and to speak of him brought it all back to her." He stares almost moodily into his glass before saying, "I know now that it was all an act. The whole time she was with me, she was plotting against Luc. She knew he had someone in his life and that he was happy. And *that* she wouldn't allow. In her mind, Lia became the cause for all of her issues."

"But if you weren't keeping her updated on Lucian's life, how was she getting the information? I know he's in the public eye some, but he's fairly private where his personal life is concerned."

Aidan actually chuckles now, although it doesn't appear he is actually amused. He runs a hand through his hair, causing it to stick up. Damn, the man looks adorable regardless. "Yeah, as it turns out, a woman I'd been seeing was Cassie's stepsister. Luc had a one-night stand with her in college, and she'd never forgiven him for it. They'd slept together again once in recent years, then he'd wanted nothing more to do with her. Cassie had no idea this woman existed since her mother left her and her father when she was young. Her father told her that she was dead, but in reality, she'd taken off and eventually remarried.

Monique found out about Cassie and went to see her while she was hospitalized. Luc had been awarded guardianship of Cassie because there was no one else who would assume the financial responsibility. He then transferred that to me when Cassie was released. Monique took us both to court and ended up taking over Cassie's care since she was a relative through her father's marriage to Cassie's mother. It's a big complicated mess, but in the end, Monique poisoned Cassie's already sick mind with more lies until she believed that Lia had taken her baby and that if she killed her, she could have Luc back and everything she'd lost."

"Holy shit." I sag back in my chair amazed at the story he's just told. I knew some of it from my father, but clearly, he'd just scratched the surface. No wonder Aidan was reeling. Not only had he lost Cassie, but he'd also dated the woman who orchestrated it all. Even though none of it was his fault, I know he's riddled with guilt. How can one person be expected to handle *that* and still go on? The fact he's here with me now is nothing short of amazing. He looks pale and dejected sending me into protective mode.

"Why don't we order a pizza to go and take it with us? I don't know about you, but I'm tired and wouldn't mind having an early night."

He shoots me a grateful look and signals for our waiter. Within fifteen minutes he's carrying a pizza box with one hand and holding on to me with the other. We both pick at our food when we get home. And by nine, we're in the bed. For the first time, we don't make love. Instead, Aidan wraps himself around my back, and we lie in silence. I'm finally lulled to sleep by the steady sound of his breathing. It seems as if I've barely been out for a few minutes before something wakes me. Then I feel the bed moving and hear Aidan mumbling under his breath before he begins shouting. "Cassie, let me in! Open the damn door!"

I roll across the bed, fumbling for the lamp on my side. I blink rapidly at the sudden glow that fills my side of the room. Aidan is moving erratically on the bed, almost as if he's waging a war against an assailant only he can see. I place my hand on his shoulder and find it dripping with sweat. "Aidan," I say softly as I give him a shake. If anything, he appears to grow even more agitated. "Aidan! Wake up, you're dreaming," I shout, and he freezes, but his eyes don't open. "It's not real, baby. You're here with me."

He's completely still for another moment before his eyes open. Without saying a word, he leaves the bed and gets to his feet. He's inches away from the door when he turns and says, "That's where you're wrong, Kara. It is very real, and I can't get it out of my fucking head." Then he's gone. I hear the front door slam, and I sag back against the sheets. The torment in his voice is my undoing, and I'm helpless to contain the flood of tears that course down my cheeks. This isn't about jealousy that he's dreaming of another woman. Actually, that has nothing to do with it. No, my emotional breakdown is caused by the realization that I've let myself care about Aidan more than I could have imagined. I'd say I'm falling in love with him, but that seems absurd after such a short time. Being as I have little experience with love, I'm not sure I'm even equipped to recognize the difference.

What I do know is that I'm the last woman he needs in his life. As far as I know, he's never had a serious relationship, so although it seems highly unlikely, what if he's also developed feelings for me? I'm physically fine right now, but what if my cancer returns? Aidan can't be expected to handle another loss in his life. Since I chose to enter into this with him without telling him the full truth, then I must also leave in the same way. Somewhere within me, I must find the courage I used to possess and return home to rebuild my life. The longer I stay here with him, the harder it will be to walk away. Even now as I think of it, I'm filled with unwelcome anguish. I wish I had never run into him at that damn bar. But how could I have possibly known we'd click almost as if he's the missing piece of me? How could fate be so cruel as to have me cross paths with him of all people? A man who could not possibly deal with the baggage that weighs so heavily on my shoulders. The writing is on the wall. These few weeks with him are all I can have. When the morning comes and I leave him asleep as I always do, I won't be coming back. And the part of me that is already grieving hopes that maybe he'll miss me just a bit too.

CHAPTER FIVE

Lucian Quinn

I'm beyond relieved that Cindy is still at lunch when I walk into the office. She'll take one look at me and know something is wrong. I may be fierce and unreadable in business, but with my assistant and mother figure, I'm an open book. There's no hiding anything from her, and as much I love the woman, today I need some time to think. I take a seat behind my desk and my hands automatically reach for the keyboard of my computer before I pull them back. I've mostly respected Aidan's wishes for the last year and kept my contact at a minimum, but what I learned today changes things. Drastically.

Lia and I try to meet for lunch at least one day a week when we can get away for an hour together. Since the addition of our daughter, Lara, those alone times are at a premium. Not that I would change anything, but I miss the easy access I once had to my wife. *In more ways than one.*

I also miss my best friend. For twelve months, I've struggled to exist without the person who's been my brother since childhood. A dozen times a day, I've picked up my phone to text or call him only to realize I can't. He hasn't been down the hall in the office he's occupied since I started Quinn Software. I haven't been able to meet him at the bar near my house where we'd dodge the overeager and slightly scary advances of Misty the bartender. He's been gone from my life as if he'd never been there.

I was walking back to the office after lunch with Lia when I ran into Aidan's parents. I felt sheepish when shaking his father's hand. I've spoken to him by phone and email but have made no effort to visit them since my best friend's departure. Quite simply, it hurts too much.

Chris Spencer used our handshake to pull me into a hug, and I felt my throat tighten. I was an asshole. How had I let so much time go by without at least inviting them over for dinner? Lia actually mentioned it on several occasions, but I always had some excuse. When I pulled back, my attention switched to Ginny Spencer. *Oh. fuck.* I knew she had some health concerns, but Chris had assured me she was doing well. One look at her and I knew that was a lie. She was so thin, so frail, and she looked as if she'd aged twenty years. She was wearing a pink bandana around her head, which only highlighted the paleness of her face. I tried to hide my shock, but I knew she saw it as I wrapped my arms gently around her small frame. Hell, I've always been a blunt man and therefore was unable to hold the words back. I looked from Chris to Ginny before saying, "Why didn't you tell me?"

They didn't bother to deny or pretend to misunderstand. Ginny put her hand on my arm and squeezed it. Her grip was surprisingly firm, which somehow made me feel better. "Don't blame Chris, Luc. It's what I wanted. If you'd known, you would have contacted Aidan, and I don't want him to know." Chris stepped closer and rubbed his wife's back before shooting me a look full of apology.

He addressed me as he always had. "Son, I know you're upset with us, but I've respected Ginny's wishes, even though I don't necessarily agree with them."

"You have cancer," I stated as I studied Ginny. "Which kind?"

"It's uterine cancer," she said calmly, almost serenely. Of course, that has always been Ginny. No matter what Aidan and I did growing up, she never raised her voice. Even when we were wrestling in the living room and accidently broke a vase her mother had left her when she passed away, she'd calmly told us to be careful of the glass on the floor. I'd seen her hands shake when she'd swept the priceless treasure up. Aidan and I had used our allowance and bought her the most beautiful one we could find to replace it. She'd cried and hugged us both tightly and declared it the best present she'd ever received. *That* was Ginny Spencer. She could always find a bright side to everything, but I couldn't help but wonder how she managed to do that now.

"Ginny, I could have helped. We can still find you the best doctors and specialists." Swallowing audibly, I said huskily, "Aidan would expect me to take care of you, and so far, I've done a crap job of it."

Chris cleared his throat, obviously emotional from the conversation. "Son, I have great insurance through my job with the state. Ginny loves her doctor, and we haven't wanted for anything. We're getting by just fine, so don't feel as if you've failed us because you haven't."

"And the prognosis?" I asked, not even sure I wanted the answer. I couldn't bear to think of losing another mother. *Dammit, Aidan, you have to come home.* His parents might mean well, but Aidan would never forgive any of us if he missed what could possibly be his last days with his mother.

Ginny looked down at her watch before saying, "I have another chemo treatment in less than an hour." She pointed across the street at the large medical building. I've walked past it a million times but have never given any particular thought to it, and now it held the key to all my hopes for Aidan and his family at that moment. "I had surgery last month, and now, I have another month of chemo. Then we'll run tests to see where I'm at. The doctor is very optimistic, though, and so far, everything has been going well."

I bit my tongue to keep from asking her what she considered "going well," because she looked so very sick to me, and nothing like the vibrant woman I have known and loved. We had talked for a few more minutes before they needed to leave for their appointment. I hugged Ginny once again. "I love you," I said softly. I could tell she was getting emotional, so I pulled away and gave her a moment to regroup. Otherwise, we'd probably both be crying on the sidewalk. Chris walked a few steps away and motioned me over while Ginny sat on a nearby bench and looked at her phone. "Please let me know if you need anything at all. I realize I haven't been around, and there's no excuse." I felt so ashamed of my failure that it was hard to meet Chris's eyes. I knew he saw everything I was thinking. How would I tell Lia? How would I admit the repercussion of my failure to her? *Fuck.*

He looked over at his wife before turning back to me. "I think you know the one thing you can do for me." I stared at him, trying to make sense of his statement. He already told me they had a good doctor and were happy with the treatment plan. *What was he talking about?* Then his cryptic words hit me.

"Aidan." Regardless of what had been said earlier, he wanted his son to know what's going on, but couldn't— *wouldn't*—betray his wife's wishes. Now, I could provide him a way around that.

He hugged me without acknowledging that I spoke. "We'd better get going. Ginny doesn't like to be late. I love you, son." He retraced his steps to his wife, and I stood frozen in place when they crossed the street and entered the door of the imposing brick building.

I made my way back to my office in a daze torn between Ginny and Chris's wishes. But in the end, was there really any choice? I failed them by staying away for so long, but that was going to change. It was time.

Time for Aidan to come home as well. He'd never recover if he lost his mother while not knowing the extent of her illness. Therefore, I tap on my keyboard and pull up my email screen. My hands hover over the keys as I ponder what to say, before finally settling on the direct approach. I've never been one for drama, so Aidan will know immediately that things are dire.

Your mother is very sick. They haven't told you the extent of it. You need to come home ASAP. Luc

I look at the flashing cursor for a few seconds before clicking on the send icon. I didn't want to mention the word cancer over email. That's something his parents should tell him in person. But if I know my friend and brother, what I have said will send him packing and on his way home very soon. After months of wanting him to come back, this is absolutely not how I saw it happening. I find no joy in the prospect of his return now. Instead of the relieved reunion I envisioned, it will only be filled with more torment for a man who has endured enough for a lifetime.

Aidan

I have no idea how long I've been sitting on the beach. But it must surely be well after midnight by now. I hadn't had a nightmare in weeks, actually since Kara began sharing my bed. The one that had woken me tonight had been so painfully vivid that my hands still shook slightly from it. Strangely enough, it was after these dreams that I usually missed home the most. Luc had a wife and baby now, but I had no doubt he'd be there for me in a moment, should I call. That is if I wasn't hiding away from the world as I was doing now. I had needed to leave, that much was still true. I wouldn't have coped if people had treated me with kid gloves and walked around me as if on eggshells.

Sympathetic glances. Halted conversations upon my entry. No. When I return, it won't be as if Cassie's death had only been a week ago. Time, and my friends, has marched on. And as much as my recovery began in solitude while being away, it is time to return. It's time to surround myself with those who understand and care about me. It's time.

I had surprised myself earlier when I told Kara about Cassie. It wasn't something I'd intended, but before I knew it, the story had spilled from my lips. And along with it, possibly a little of the pain I'd been carrying around for so long. At least that's what I thought. But then the fucking nightmare had me teetering on the edge once again.

I pull my cell phone from my pocket, not knowing why I'd even bothered to grab it on the way out the door. I click on the screen and then go to my photos. At times when I am feeling lost and lonely, I flip through the dozens of images of my parents, Luc, and the few of him with Lia. I also have a couple of Lara when she was born right before I left town. Tonight, though, instead of feeling better, they just make me feel worse. It has taken over a year, but I think I'm finally ready to go home. It's been too long since I've seen my beautiful mother or laughed with my father. And I damn sure need my friend and brother.

Then my thoughts turn to Kara. I never planned on her, but I'm not ready to walk away from her. Will she agree to go back with me? We don't even have what I'd call a relationship. We spend the evenings together, and with the exception of tonight, we fuck—a lot. We've never spoken of anything past the here and now, but I know she's dealing with more than she'll admit. I see the haunted look in her eyes when she doesn't think I'm watching her. She's a puzzle I've become obsessed with solving. There are so many contradictions between her words and actions. She may be a mystery, but what I do know is that in a short time, it's become hard to imagine not sleeping beside her each night. I'll talk to her in the morning before she can disappear for the day. I'm getting to my feet when I notice an email notification on the phone screen. Since only a few people have the address, days can go by between correspondences. I almost leave it 'til morning, but then I go ahead and click it just in case my father has more news of my mother.

I see Luc's name and relax a bit. He does check in from time to time to let me know he's ready for me to come home. Looks like this might be his lucky week. I open the email and feel the panic return: **Your mother is very sick. They haven't told you the extent of it. You need to come home ASAP. Luc**

Fuck me! Despite my father's reassurances, I knew something wasn't right. It may sound crazy, but his words were strained, and I could almost see the effort he was making to keep things light. I've pulled up my parents' number, and my finger is hovering over the send button before I know it. Something stops me, though. A middle-of-the-night call from their absent son is the last thing they need. If I pack and head out within the next hour, I can be home early in the morning. My running days are over. I have family and friends who depend on me, and I've let them down for long enough. I rush across the sand and barrel in the front door, not bothering to be quiet. There's no way I'm leaving without talking to Kara, so waking her isn't something I try to avoid.

The lamp on my side of the bed is burning, and Kara is on her side facing me when I walk in. "Are you okay?" she asks in that husky voice I've come to crave.

"Not really," I answer truthfully, as I make my way to the closet and pull my suitcase from it. "Princess, I've got to go home tonight. Luc emailed to tell me that my mother is really sick despite what they've been telling me."

I hear the bed move, and then her hand is on my arm. "Don't worry about the house. I can lock up if you leave the key. What else do I need to take care of?"

That stops me in the act of tossing clothes on the bed. I turn and cup her face in my hand. "Babe, I want you to come back with me. I realize we haven't discussed anything more than the here and now, but I can't imagine leaving you here and walking away. We both live in the same city so it's not as if you're relocating."

I feel the distance opening between us as her head drops, and she takes a few steps back. "I—I can't go back yet, Aidan." I open my mouth to argue, but she quickly adds, "I just need a few more weeks. You don't have time to discuss this. Let's get you packed and on the road. You'll need some time with your parents. I'll finish my vacation and be close behind you, okay?"

She's saying all the right things, and despite not understanding why, I don't believe any of them. I'm being placated, and I hate that. But right now, I don't have time to call her on it, and she knows it. I reach out and pull her back to me, enfolding her in my arms. "Don't you fucking run from me, princess," I murmur against the crown of her head. She stiffens before relaxing once again. Whether she knows it or not, that little tell confirms everything I already suspected. She has no intention of coming to me. Dammit, I know she wants to—I can literally feel her inner turmoil—so what is holding her back? I want to demand an explanation, but even if I took the time now, I know it wouldn't get me anywhere. She's locked up tight. If I corner her, she'll do nothing but blow sunshine up my ass and agree to any plea or demand I make. So I tilt her head until I can take possession of her mouth. It's a hard, deep kiss filled with my frustration. She returns the rough embrace without complaint. Her tongue clashes with mine as we wage some kind of silent war with each other. When I pull away suddenly, looking down at her, I see a deep sadness in her eyes. *Shit.* She's already gone. The only thing that gives me the strength to finish packing and leave is knowing that I'll find her. She has too many ties to my friends. She won't be able to hide from me forever. She's the first woman in my life other than Cassie who I've developed real feelings for. And I'm not going to let her turn her back on me just yet.

She tosses on her shirt and follows me out to my car, standing quietly as I stow my case in the backseat. "I hope your mom's okay," she says softly as her fingers twist nervously together in front of her.

I hand her the key to the house before dropping one last kiss onto her lips. "Don't take too long to figure it out, Kara. I'll be waiting." I don't bother waiting for a reply. I'm in my car and moving down the driveway before I see her glance up. She looks so lost and vulnerable. I desperately want to go back and demand she get into the car, but how much of a hypocrite can I be? It's taken me a year and a family emergency to reach this point. Who am I to deny her at least some of the time she so obviously needs? There is a moment of dread so intense it makes my chest hurt. The last time I left a woman who I cared about behind, she died. I open my window and draw air into my suddenly burning lungs. *This isn't the same thing* I repeat to myself as I stare straight ahead. As the miles between us begin to lengthen, I slowly relax. When I've found out what's going on with my mother and things are settled there, I'll find Kara. Instinctively, I know she won't be at home, and she'll leave the beach soon. I'm a man with resources, and I'll use them. And if she doesn't like it? Too fucking bad.

Kara

As Aidan's car makes the turn onto the highway, I drop to my knees. He's gone. I'm always the one to leave first in the morning, yet this time, he does. I don't know why I'm acting like the love of my life just dumped me. This was the end of the road for us anyway; I'd already made the decision. My emotions are raw, and I feel as if I've been abandoned, which is absurd considering he asked me to go with him. *He wants more time with me.* And I lied to his face as I assured him I'd be back in Asheville soon.

The cool beach breeze sends a chill through me, and I get to my feet and walk wearily back into the house. There's so much of Aidan here that I almost can't stand it. Maybe it's my imagination, but the air seems heavy with his scent, which both comforts and repels me. A part of me wants to pack and follow him immediately, but I can't. If it hurts this much to lose him now, allowing myself—and possibly him—to form further attachment would be devastating.

I make my way to the bedroom and curl up on the top of the covers. I should leave now, but I allow myself to have these last hours in the place where Aidan Spencer came so very close to stealing my heart. Before I know what I'm doing, I've cupped my reconstructed breast in my hand. It's ridiculous, but I blame it for so much. This imposter that has taken over my life and sent me into a tailspin of depression and despair. For one insane moment, I feel the almost overwhelming urge to find a knife and hack it off as if everything will go back to normal after that. *I hate it. Hate. It. I want my life back. If only cutting it off would give me that.*

But it won't. I'll never be the girl I was before breast cancer, and this carefully constructed breast that I hold such disdain for did nothing wrong. It simply keeps me from feeling like less of a woman. And God forbid I go around with only one breast. That might make everyone around me uncomfortable. *Poor Kara Jacks. She only has one good tit now.* My thoughts are so irrational that I can't help but laugh. It's a crazy sound in the silent room. I'm a survivor; I'm supposed to be stronger than this. I should be speaking about the power of positive thinking at events. Visiting the hospitals to encourage others battling cancer and handing out those little pink ribbons. Sometimes, I think the fact I lived was a mistake. Shouldn't remission be reserved for someone who would make the most of their life instead of cowering away from the world? Just how long is this pity party going to last before I am forced to admit that I'm plain fucking nuts now? *Yes, that's right, God, you wasted your healing power on me. I can't figure out how not to be a victim.*

I'm startled out of my dark thoughts by the text tone on my phone. I fumble around on the nightstand and hit a button to light the screen. When I see that it's a message from Aidan, I eagerly open it. ***Miss you already, princess. Soon.***

Damn you. Missing you already, princess. How is it possible that I miss him too? I'm not a princess. I may have once thought I lived a charmed life and could leave my ivory tower on the rare occasion, but I'd never been a snob. I'd never held myself above others. Right now, my crown has well and truly slipped. I sniff and know that yet another round of tears are imminent. Why couldn't he be the playboy he's reputed to be? He could have fucked my brains out and then moved on. But nooo, he had to turn into this perfect man along the way. Sweet, funny, dirty, and possessive. I doubt there's a woman out there who doesn't have most of those things on her wish list. I picked him up that first night thinking he'd make me forget everything. The man was supposed to be a god in the sack, and I'd been attracted to him since our first meeting at Luc and Lia's wedding. That had been right after I'd finished my chemo and had decided to dye my naturally blond hair almost black. There had been a moment that day when our eyes had connected and lingered for just a second longer than the standard greeting. He had been so solemn, so sad, even though it was his best friend's wedding day. I'd laughed at all the right moments and smiled when I had to, but I'd felt the same. Shortly after that, I'd heard through the family grapevine that he'd left town for an unknown amount of time. Even then, not knowing his entire story, I'd understood his need to flee because I'd been fighting the same urge. Who would have ever guessed that a year later our paths would cross many miles from home? Again, the word fate or even destiny comes to mind. Which is probably pretty accurate because that bitch isn't finished with me yet. Dangling someone like Aidan in front of me knowing I can't keep him is about as cruel as the fear I have that my cancer will return . . . Only that time I won't be one of the "lucky ones."

CHAPTER SIX

Aidan

The sun is just beginning to rise when I drive down the street I grew up on. It's an old, established neighborhood with some newer houses beginning to replace ones that had seen better days. People rarely wanted to spend the time or money to refurbish anymore. It was an impatient world, and everyone demanded immediate results. Of course, it didn't matter that a new build took longer. That didn't really enter into it. The modern one-size-fits-all was better to most than its drafty, classic counterpart.

I spot my parents' white Victorian surrounded by, of course, a white picket fence. Its style has been featured in countless movies, and it's been the inspiration behind fairy tales and love stories. The porch light glows in the early morning light as if it had been expecting my arrival all along. *Home.* Our initials are carved in the oak tree out back, and under it, two dogs that had died of old age are buried. I rub a small scar under my chin and grin as I remember Luc and I having the bright idea to ride our bikes off the steep porch. Luc's had been fine, but mine had made a sideways flip that had ended with me in the emergency room. I'd proudly told everyone at school about my five stitches. It had actually been two, but that hadn't sounded as badass, so I'd embellished just a tad.

I step out of the car, closing the door behind me quietly, loathe to disturb the peace of the moment. I know that as soon as I make my presence known, it will be gone. Despite feeling right that I'm home, I'm almost fearful of moving from the spot I'm frozen in. My mind is urging me toward the front door, but fear is holding me captive with one hand still on the door handle as if preparing for a quick escape. I'm still mired in doubt when I hear footsteps behind me. I swing around and am shocked to see my father walking up the driveway toward me. His hands are buried in his pockets, and his gait is heavier than I've ever seen before. With lines in his face that were not previously there, he looks as if he's aged several years since I've been gone. I also notice that for all of my shock, he doesn't seem surprised to see me. "Son," he says simply, as he closes the last of the distance between us and pulls me into his arms. "I've missed you," I hear him mutter as I return his embrace.

When we part, I speak the obvious. "You knew I was on my way."

He shrugs before giving a single nod. "I had no way of knowing for certain, but I felt sure that Luc would contact you. Your mother likes to sleep a little later these days. Why don't we walk down the street to Joe's and get a cup of coffee? She's going to be so excited when she sees you that this may be the only alone time we get today, and I'd like to spend a little time with my son."

A million questions are on the tip of my tongue, but I push them back. My dad has never been one for blurting anything out, and that hasn't changed. I know he wants to talk about Mom while she's not around, so I fall into step with him. I'm thankful for the small talk about the neighbors as we walk toward the old café at the end of our street. The air inside is thick with the smell of coffee and grease as we take a seat across from each other on the stiff and sticky vinyl. I can't help but grin as I see the miniature jukebox on the table. I'm tempted to pop in a quarter just to see if it actually works, but figure it's a little too early for Elvis or Patsy Cline. A quick glance shows that Joe hasn't bothered to update his music selection in years. A gum-chewing waitress, who looks bored with life, sets our hot cups of coffee down and takes off before we change our mind about ordering food. I take a cautious sip and wince. Just as strong as I remember. Hell, for all I know, this is the same damn pot from a year ago. "So what's going on?" I ask my dad point-blank. I think we've covered the casual chitchat portion by now. "Your mother has uterine cancer." He doesn't bother to act ignorant. He's always been the direct sort and now is no exception. "She had surgery, and they performed a complete hysterectomy, along with removing the ovaries and her tubes. There are so other medical terms thrown in, but that's the gist of it. It has also spread to the lymph nodes in that area so they were taken out as well. Now, she's in the middle of her six months of chemo."

And for the second time in a year, the bottom has just fallen completely from my world. *She's in the middle of her six months of chemo. She's had three months of chemo, and I haven't been here. Fuck!*

My mother has always been invincible in my eyes. I can hardly fathom her sick with the flu much less fucking cancer. I feel the urge to run away from it all again, but I can't. Doing that in the first place may have well cost me precious time with the woman I love more than life itself. On the heels of that is anger, and even though I know I have no one to blame but myself, I still find myself lashing out. "Why in the hell didn't you tell me? You said she'd had some tests done ages ago. I kept asking about it, and you glossed it over, even blamed it on hormones at one point. Were you just planning to eventually send me an email and say, 'Merry Christmas. Oh, by the way, your mother died of cancer last week.'?" The few other customers turn to stare as my voice rises, but I couldn't give a fuck. Let them have a show with their breakfast this morning.

He pinches the bridge of his nose then looks up to return my stare. I see it then.

Complete and utter devastation.

But it's the fact he appears so lost that scares the hell out of me. He's the man with all the answers. If I'd listened to him years ago, I'd have avoided a world of hurt with Cassie. I see none of that calm confidence now, though. "I'm sorry, Aidan," he finally says. "I wanted to tell you so much, but your mother was against it. She wanted you to have this time for yourself. She knew how much you were hurting and didn't want to cause you more stress. I promise you I tried to get her to reconsider so many times. She flat out threatened to leave me at one point if I betrayed her confidence. And even though I don't think she meant that, it did show me how strongly she felt about her decision." His hands shake so badly that coffee sloshes over the rim of his cup. "But I'd been wavering lately. It killed me each time you asked about her, and I had to pretend things were fine. When we ran into Lucian yesterday, I wanted to drop to my knees and thank God for showing me a way to contact you without breaking my word to your mother."

My shoulders slouch forward as the anger drains from my body. He's hurting; it's clear to see. My parents are the true embodiment of soul mates. Of course, this is hitting him hard, and *I'm* throwing a tantrum because I abandoned them and they didn't beg me to come back when something happened. The blame here is mine, and it's unfair to pretend otherwise. I need to be part of the solution now, instead of the problem I've been for so long. I place my hand on his arm, giving it a squeeze. "I'm sorry, Dad. That was an asshole thing to say, and I didn't mean it."

He puts his hand over mine, squeezing it tightly. "I know, son. She didn't want you to return home to this. I believe she kept hoping it would all be over, and she'd be well again before you came back. You know how damned stubborn she is. She's just been waiting for the tide to turn and that exact thing to happen." *Yes, I am fully aware of her stubbornness. I am most definitely her son.*

"What are her doctors saying?" I ask, almost afraid to hear the answer. What if there's no hope? I've heard of people who find out they have cancer and are dead a month later. She's my mother, for fuck's sake, not some sad statistic to be recorded in a book somewhere.

"As we told Luc, we both really like her doctor. They've been aggressive in her treatment and are optimistic about the outcome. Right now, we're doing everything we can to keep her healthy and minimize everyday risks such as her catching a cold or the flu from someone. Little things like that are her biggest threat at this point. The chemo has lowered her immune system so much that she's at risk every time she leaves the house. Hell, I can bring it home from work, Walmart, or anywhere, and not even know it." Giving a thin smile, he adds, "Needless to say, we've gone through a lot of Lysol."

I hate to ask this next question, but it will tell me so much more than the facts he's presented so far. It will also be the most difficult, probably for both of us. "So I know her doctor's opinion now, but what do YOU think? You know Mom better than anyone does, and you're privy to more than they are in those brief appointments. How is she really doing, Dad?"

His eyes fall, and he appears to wilt before me. If I thought he looked several years older before, I now think it's more like ten years. "I'm not sure, son," he admits. "She's so damn strong that what would break some people barely slows her stride. But I've never seen her this tired or this frail. She looks as if a stiff wind would blow her over. You need to prepare yourself for the fact that she's lost a lot of weight." Then swallowing audibly, he adds, "And most of her hair." His eyes glisten with tears at this point, and I know it has nothing to do with vanity. He wouldn't care if my mother were bald, short, tall, heavy, or thin. What must pain him is seeing her change so drastically due to the beast living within her. His voice is hoarse now as he fights to control his emotions. "I want to say that everything is going to be okay because that's exactly what she's going to tell you. And I hope to God she's right. But this has hit her hard, and each day, I see her lose a little more of herself to this fucking disease!"

With first my profane outburst and now his, we're attracting attention in the dingy diner. My father isn't one for the F-word, so it says a lot about his frustration and fear over my mother's condition. I pull my wallet from my pocket and toss some bills on the table. "Why don't we head home and see if Mom is up yet?" We both get to our feet; I throw my arm over his shoulders, giving him a side hug, and we make our way back to my childhood home. I don't miss the irony—for the first time in my life, I'm the one offering moral support, and he's the one leaning on me. But despite his dire warnings, ten minutes later when I'm folding my stick-thin mother in my arms, I'm reeling. *Fuck. Fuck me. How? God, this hurts so much. Why her? Why fucking her?* I'm grateful her head is somewhere around my chest, and she can't see the look of agonizing disbelief on my face. When I left home, she had thick brown hair and a healthy glow. Now, she's hunched over, bald, and saying she weighed a hundred pounds would be generous. I have a sinking feeling that she's below that. Her once vibrant blue eyes, which always sparkled like sapphires, are now a muted color, and her few laugh lines have been replaced with wrinkles that look as if they're relentlessly claiming every remaining smooth curve of her face. *Where in the fuck is my mother and who is the shell that has replaced her?*

But then she cups my face and strokes my cheek as she's always done and I see her there. Cancer is laying waste to her body, but the woman I love is still alive and buried under it all. *Don't cry,* I chant in my mind over and over.

She knows me so well, though. She sees that I'm struggling as she pulls away to study me. I have no clue what to say. What is the appropriate way to make conversation with your dying mother? Because as morbid as it may sound, that's exactly the conclusion I've formed. Like Dad, I can't see a rainbow with puppies waiting at the other end here. Granted, I don't really have any experience with people who are going through chemo. Maybe they all look like this, and then later on, they go back to normal. I simply can't wrap my head around what's happening here, though. "My baby," she says softly, and that's it. I crumple at her feet and sob exactly like the infant she just called me. She lowers herself to the floor with me and pulls me close, stroking my hair as she's always soothed me when I was upset. "Shhh, don't cry, sweetheart. You're home now, and this is a happy occasion. I've missed your face so much." The guilt I feel at her last words is strong enough to suffocate me. Having been absent, I may have very well missed the last good parts of my mother's life.

My father has left the room. After our emotional talk, I'm sure this was more than he could bear. "I'm so sorry, Mom," I manage to get out as she rocks us both back and forth with her frail body. I have no clue how she even has the strength to move herself, much less me. "Why didn't you tell me what was going on? I would have come back right away."

We settle back against the front of the sofa with our hands clasped tightly together. "One day, you'll understand, honey. But parents, especially mothers, have a need to protect their children. You've been through so much in the last year, and you needed the time to grieve."

"But what if that had cost me the chance to see you again? To spend time with you?" I ask, still frustrated that no one told me something so important. This wasn't like missing a birthday or a job promotion.

"I would have never left this earth without saying goodbye to you," she says as if it's the most logical answer in the world.

I roll my eyes and drop my head back against the sofa cushions. "You know sometimes you don't get to make that decision, right?" I point out wryly. "Even you're not the Almighty, all powerful every day."

"Who says?" She laughs as she leans her head against my shoulder. "When it comes to you, my will is stronger than anything this universe can toss at me. Of course, it did throw Luc directly in our path yesterday so maybe it got tired of my delays." We talk for a while longer before I notice the lengthening lapses between her words. I turn my head and see her eyelashes fluttering before a big yawn escapes. "Sorry," she says sheepishly. "You just got home, and I don't want to take my usual morning nap, but it looks like my body has other plans."

"I'm a little tired too from the drive," I admit even though I would have gladly stayed. I get to my feet and help her up. Her weight is so slight that it again drives home to me how precarious her condition is right now. "How about I come by this evening and bring dinner with me? I can pick up your favorite Italian from Leo's."

"That sounds great, honey," she murmurs as I drop a kiss on her forehead. She turns and makes her way down the hallway toward the bedrooms. A lump forms in my throat as I notice her unsteady gait. *Where has the mother I left behind gone?* I'm with my dad. I absolutely loathe this fucking disease.

Dad is raking in the front yard when I step outside. I tell him the plans for dinner, and he says he's going in to get ready for work. He's hired a sitter to be with Mom during the day because he needs to work to keep his health care coverage. I make a mental note to discuss their finances with him that evening. I know it'll be a touchy subject, but with everything else they're dealing with, I don't want money to be another point of stress. I'm not rolling in it, but I've made enough from investments and my salary to want for nothing.

I get in the car and almost without thought head toward Quinn Software. I wasn't lying when I said I was tired, but I want to see Luc. Only the man I think of as a brother could possibly understand the anguish I feel at the thought of losing the woman who defined so much of our lives.

A sense of rightness fills me as I walk through the doors of the software company that my friend built from the ground up. It's been my second home ever since. The security guard does a double take when he spots me. While Luc is well liked by all his employees and is always friendly, I usually take it one step further. I'm a phenomenal salesman and customer liaison because I have the personality for it. I have the ability to make people feel instantly comfortable. Mom always said people were drawn to me like bees to honey. My dad used to say I could sell shit to a manure farmer. I think maybe it's a little of both. It had certainly served me well in business and with women. Well, most women anyway.

"Mr. Spencer! It's great to see you again," he says enthusiastically.

I reach out to shake hands and clap him on the shoulder. "Thanks, Calvin. How's the family doing? Bet the little one is getting big now. Probably into everything." He pulls his phone out and shows me a picture of his smiling family. I have to give it to old Calvin; his wife is hot. He definitely married up there. Their kid, unfortunately, looks more like Calvin than his mother. Hopefully, that'll change for him in the future. "You're a lucky man." I grin. "Is Luc in yet?"

Nodding, Calvin says, "He went up about ten minutes ago."

"Good deal. I'm going to surprise him; he doesn't know I'm back yet."

I'm strangely nervous as the floors whiz by. Luckily, only a handful of people have the code to this private elevator, so I don't have to make more small talk. I haven't slept for nearly twenty-four hours and just endured the most soul-crushing moment learning of my mother's cancer. I'm exhausted. Physically. Emotionally. I take a deep breath as I step out and turn the corner. Then almost as if in slow motion, I see the exact moment Cindy spots me. She freezes in her chair before her hand comes up to cover her mouth. She's been with Luc for a long time and mothers both of us. Naturally, we grumble about it, but we love it and her. She flies around the desk with impressive speed for a woman in her fifties. I'd never say that aloud because she'd probably beat my ass. Did I mention I'm a little scared of her? Her usual composure seems to desert her, and she's literally tackling me in the foyer. "Aidan! You're home. No one told me—wait, does Luc know? I want to hug you and smack you upside your head at the same time." Luckily, the affectionate part of the threat wins out, and she enfolds me in her embrace.

"It's good to see you, beautiful," I say sincerely. Again, I'm a little choked up and have to blink rapidly to clear my eyes. Less than a few hours back and I've turned into a sniveling pussy.

"Must you paw my wife, boy?" an amused voice says from behind me. I spin around to see Luc's driver, Sam, standing there with his hands on his hips. "I knew it had to be you." He shrugs. "Cindy will hug only a few people in this building. I just saw Max downstairs a few minutes ago, and Luc doesn't have those girly curls you're sporting in your hair now."

"Ass," I say affectionately as we shake hands and perform our version of a bro-hug. "Wait—did you say wife?" I look from Cindy to him. She's blushing like a teenager just busted by her parents, and he looks like the only cock in a hen house. "Well, I'll be damned. You closed the deal." I grin as I slug him on the shoulder. "You better not screw this up," I add sternly, "and make sure you use protection." Cindy gasps in horror, but Sam only laughs.

"You're so bad." She laughs. "It's been nice without you here. Forget what I said about missing you."

I throw my arm around her and lower my head to whisper, "We're playing it cool, right? Sam doesn't know I'm the backup plan, does he?" I make a show of zipping my lips and throwing away the key. She promptly sticks a surprisingly bony finger in my side, and I move away, throwing my hands up in surrender.

Her face is suddenly serious as she says, "He's been lost with you, Aidan. At least once a day, I walk into his office, and he's staring out the window. He has that look, and I know he's thinking of you. It's as if he's just been running on autopilot since you left. You took the heart right out of this place, and we've all felt the loss." She pats my shoulder as if I'm her wayward child. "Now, I know you did what you needed to do, and he understands that too. But you boys are a part of each other. Always thick as thieves. Max has tried to step in, but he's grieved for you. He's going to be so happy and surprised to see you're back." And like that, all three of us are sniffling. Sam and I manage to keep it together, but Cindy is crying, and I feel like a selfish bastard all over again. *Yes. The decision to come back now is the right one.*

Obviously, Luc hasn't told her about my mother, so I do. Cindy is family to me as well, and I don't want to keep anything else from her. "Luc won't be surprised to see me. I'm pretty sure he's been expecting me all morning."

She actually looks a tad disappointed. "Oh, you already let him know you were coming? Well, that's okay. He'll still be happy to see your face."

I settle on the corner of her desk as Sam takes a seat across from us. "Luc emailed me yesterday to tell me that my mother is very sick, and I needed to come home. My dad had mentioned her having tests but assured me that things were fine. However, Luc saw them yesterday and knew they weren't."

Cindy's eyes are so big on her face that I'm afraid for a moment they'll actually explode. "Is she all right? Can I do anything to help out?" And that right there is one of a million things I love about Cindy. She's always putting others first without a thought for herself.

"She has cancer," I say quietly. The words sound so horrible on my tongue that I find myself grimacing against the bad taste it leaves in my mouth. I hear Sam's sharply indrawn breath, but other than that, we all sit in silence for a few moments.

Cindy rubs my leg soothingly. "I know this is hard for you to talk about, but I want you to know that we're here for you and your parents. Day or night, whatever you need. I'll be praying that God heals her and keeps your family strong."

Before I can reply, the door behind us opens, and Luc stands in the doorway. He freezes for a moment when he sees me before a huge grin breaks out. "It's about fucking time," he says gruffly, and I hear Cindy clucking her tongue at his profanity as we clasp each other in yet another hug. I haven't been hugged this much since that threesome at the beach the first month I was there. Well, except with Kara. An unexpected pang of emotion grips me as I think of her. With everything that's happened this morning, I've been too distracted to dwell on the woman I left behind. Fuck. I *won't* see her today or hold her tonight. We've only been together for such a short time, but she's well and truly under my skin. I'm brought back from my thoughts, and Luc slaps me across the back—possibly a little harder than necessary—and adds, "I've missed you, brother." I see the questions and worry in his eyes and know he's wondering if I've been to my parents' yet. Being the friend he is, though, he doesn't want to mention it in front of Sam and Cindy, unaware they already know.

I fall back on my trademark humor to lighten the moment. "You're not going to cry or anything, are you? I swear you're such a chick since you got married." I smirk.

Luc shakes his head, pulling me into his office by my shirt. "Just as big of an asshole as ever, I see. Good to know some things don't change, right, Cindy?" he throws over his shoulder. She clucks her tongue and then shuts the door behind us. Instead of going to his place behind the desk as he normally would, he goes to the seating area in the corner and reclines on the leather sofa. I take a nearby chair, and we both relax, no doubt thinking of the million times we've done this before. He studies his hands for a moment then utters, "I'm damn glad to see you, but I never wanted to bring you back under these circumstances."

I'd suddenly like nothing better than a cigarette. I've never been a hardcore smoker, but in times of stress, it gives me something else to focus on. When I first left Asheville after Cassie's death, I was up to a pack a day. Then after a while, I got some semblance of control and cut the amount way back. It dawns on me that I haven't smoked at all since I met Kara. Hell, until this very moment, I haven't realized that. Never wanted one and didn't miss it. Apparently, she was good for me in many ways. "I was actually thinking of coming back soon before this came up. Thank you for letting me know about my mom," I say sincerely. "I don't know how much longer they would have waited had you not run into them."

Luc nods then shifts uncomfortably. "I let you down there. I should have been checking on them regularly while you were gone. We did talk on the phone some, but I never once went by their house in the whole time you were away. If I had, we would have found this out sooner."

He looks consumed by guilt, which is crazy to me considering they're my parents, and I'm the one who basically cut ties and ran. That's Luc, though. Even when we were kids, he always assumed responsibility for everyone else, so I know this must be tearing him up inside. "Don't take this on yourself; it wasn't your job to take care of everyone I left behind. That's on me. When you found out there was a problem, you contacted me right away, and here I am. Now, stop with all the fucking whining and tell me how things have been here."

He chuckles at my insult and the mood lightens. That's the usual dynamic of our relationship. He obsesses, and I provide the comic relief. I'll admit that sometimes I'm in no mood to joke around, but I think we both need it today. "Things are moving along. We've closed the deals that you had in the works and added a few more to the pot. Max took over some of that, but the amount of bitching he does is unbelievable. Hey, wait. You read my email about him and Rose, right?"

"Yeah"—I nod—"can't say I'm surprised. Those two were always gonna end up together at some point. I gather it wasn't all easy going, but at least it worked out. Have they gotten married yet?"

"Nope, not yet"—Luc grins—"but Max is tired of waiting. I wouldn't be surprised if it happens soon." In an abrupt subject change that Luc is so fond of, he asks, "How are you really? You said you were thinking of coming home, so I assume things are—better? Or at least more bearable."

I run a hand through my hair as I organize my thoughts. "I don't know if I've made my peace with everything that happened and all the wasted years, but I think I've come to accept that I can't do anything at this point to change the past. It simply is what it is. I'll always think 'what-if,' but at the end of the day, I'm powerless to go back. I wondered if I'd ever be able to live in this city again with the myriad of memories here, but this is my home. I know it'll be hard for a while, but I can't leave my family behind again."

Luc sits forward, clasping his hands together. "Aidan, I owe you more than I can ever repay . . ." he begins before I

hold up a hand to stop him. I know he's referring to the fact
that I saved Lia from Cassie that day. Would I do it again?
Absolutely. Will it haunt me until the day I die? You better
fucking believe it. I've come to realize that one person was
going to die, and I chose to save the innocent one who was
carrying my best friend's child. Of course, at the time, I
thought I had a chance to get them both out alive. But there
was no choice, not when I saw Lia on the ground. *Fuck.* I
thought she was already dead. And all I could think about
was Luc. *He wouldn't have recovered if she hadn't lived.
There was no choice.* Sometimes, doing the right thing can
mean losing a part of yourself in the process. You can only
pray that eventually some of the pieces will come together
once again, and you'll be able to look yourself in the mirror
without choking on the guilt. Seeing Luc so love and full of
life . . . yeah, I made the right call.

"You've paid your dues, Luc. Cassie tortured you for
years and took your son away. It's only right that she give
you back some of what you lost." He looks startled by my
statement as if he'd never considered such a thing. "I
wouldn't change anything from that moment," I assure him.
"I would always save Lia. Cassie wreaked havoc wherever
she went, and in the end, it killed her. If she'd made it out
that day, we would all be wondering what the hell would
happen next. The fucking sad fact is that she was destined
to be a statistic from the time she was born." My throat
tightens as I add, "I wasn't *in love* with her. I know that
now. I loved her, I always will, but I have to move on from
feeling guilty. Otherwise, I'll lose my mind right along
with her, and I'll be damned if I let that happen. I made the
right choice, Luc."

He shocks me speechless when he says, "Damn, what I
wouldn't give for a line right about now." I guess while I
had my urge to smoke, he was fighting his own for his old
vice—cocaine. To my knowledge, he's been clean for
almost two years now. Since he fell in love with Lia. If I
knew nothing else about his wife, that would be enough to

make me love her. He'd been snorting for years to deal with the shit Cassie had put him through. He'd managed to build an empire and thrive while keeping his addiction mostly secret. I, of course, knew, and it possibly made me a shitty friend, but I never tried to talk him into getting help. Hell, I understood why he needed it and figured if he was fully functional on it, then what was the harm? I realize now that my thought process was probably a bit skewed, but I also knew that you had to *want* to stop the destructive behavior before you actually could. Otherwise, you're going through the motions with no dedication behind it. Something else I'm well acquainted with. *How could one woman wreak so much havoc in the lives of two very different men? How did we allow that to happen?*

"You'd better not let a certain little blonde hear you say that." I laugh as he grimaces. "How's Lia doing? I know you mentioned she was running a company with Lee." It was still hard for me to reconcile that Lee Jacks was Lia's long-lost father. It was a well-known fact that he'd operated in gray areas for years although nothing had ever been proven. He seemed to be crazy about Lia, though, so I was willing to overlook anything else I'd heard. Rumors and innuendo were always ugly, even when I was certain some truth was thrown in.

His eyes soften, and he gets that damn whipped look he always does when he talks about her. Fuck, I never actually thought I'd see the day, but it suits him. "She's amazing. I know she's still dealing with a lot of baggage from her stepfather's attack, but the fact that he's dead, and she doesn't have to look over her shoulder any longer helps. Plus, Lee bought the company I was telling you about, and she's engrossed in helping him run it. Rose working with her now doesn't hurt any I'm sure."

The lump is back in my throat when I ask, "And the little one? How is Lara doing? I can't believe how much she's growing. Thanks for sending the pictures; I enjoyed the hell out of them even if I didn't always say it."

"Hey, you might have been gone, but you weren't forgotten," he assures me. "And Lara is great. She's walking and into damn near everything. It takes me five minutes just to pry the damn toilet open now since some kind of lock is on the lid. I figure one day, she and I will piss our pants at the same time."

I toss my head back, laughing at his words. I can just imagine my previously hardcore bachelor friend trying to live in his baby-proofed home. I bet it's freaking hysterical. "I want to see them both soon," I say. "Hopefully, not on the evening you and Lara have your future toilet miss."

"Just let me know when," he says, and then his expression goes somber. "I know you're going to want to spend time with your parents. How was your mom this morning?"

I pinch the bridge of my nose, one of my nervous tics that I've never been able to stop. Somehow, it always seems to ground me when I'm gathering my thoughts. Then I find myself saying something that even shocks me. "She's dying, Luc." I hear his sudden intake of breath as I continue. "No, she didn't say that and neither did my father. They didn't have to. It's not even the fact that she looks frail and sunken. It was what I saw in her eyes. In one unguarded moment when she didn't have her parental shield up, the truth was there and so was her acceptance. She's going through the motions and having chemo, but she fully expects to die. And what scares the fuck out of me is that you and I both know my mother is never wrong. I don't think she would be putting herself through these treatments if not for my dad and me. This is for us, but she has no expectations that it will change anything." I'm amazed that I manage to get it all out without breaking down. A part of me is still removed from what's happening as if I'm discussing someone else's mother. I think it's the only way I can deal with the horror of what's happening.

"Holy fucking shit," Luc hisses and sags back in his seat. He grips a handful of hair, looking as if he'll pull it out at any moment. "Fucking hell!" He knows my mother well enough not to argue with what I said. She was always one step ahead of us whenever we were trying to get away with something, and my father often joked about her freaky intuition. I don't think she's ever made a prediction that didn't come true at some point. And even though she didn't verbalize what I said, she might as well have. Her eyes have always been the window to her soul if you paused long enough to look into them. Of course, she could also see into mine, so as I got older and had perhaps a little more to hide, I tried to keep those direct looks to a minimum. Fuck, why hadn't I done that earlier? But I'd instinctively sought hers out, looking for a truth I would only find there. Apparently, I hadn't processed it until just now. "We'll get her the best doctors, man. I'll get on it right away. The survival rate for cancer is higher than ever. We can still turn this around," he says urgently. I wonder if he has any idea how desperate he sounds as he continues to tick off an internal list he believes would save the woman our hearts both claim as our mother.

When he's run out of steam, I say, "I'm going to her next appointment with her. I should know more then. Tonight, I'm picking up dinner from Leo's and taking it over. That is one of her favorite places, and God knows she needs to eat something."

Looking at me as if I'm a ticking time bomb, Luc says angrily, "I'm so fucking angry, Aidan. Your mom. When I told Lia last night . . . Well, you can imagine her reaction. She knows how much I love your mom. I just keep asking why. Why fucking her? You're taking this so well, while I'm freaking the fuck out. How is that possible?"

I look down for a moment before admitting, "I have no idea. As long as I keep moving and don't focus on it, I'm okay. The minute I let it in, though, I'm screwed, and I won't be of any help to her that way. The last time that happened, I left town for a year. That luxury is no longer available to me." We talk quietly for a while longer about business, leaving the personal stuff behind by unspoken agreement. We're both at our limit today. I tell him I'd like to start back to work but will need to schedule around my mother's needs, which of course is no problem at all.

I go through a round of goodbyes that are almost as long and tearful as the hellos before I'm once again standing on the sidewalk in front of Quinn Software. I can hardly wrap my head around everything that's transpired in such a short amount of time. As I push my hands into my front pockets, I again think of Kara. I had checked my phone on the way down from Luc's office, and there'd been no reply to my previous text. I guess she's as good as telling me that whatever we had is over. I can't help but worry about her, though, being there all alone. With that in mind, I shoot off another text. *If nothing else, princess, let me know you're all right. I'm worried about you.*

Within seconds, a brief reply comes through. *I'm fine. Thx for checking.* And that's it. No attempts at keeping the conversation going and no questions about how I'm doing. *I had told her about my mom.* I walk toward my car, running a hand through my hair. *Thx for checking.* She had seemed jealous over Brandy but maybe I had misinterpreted that. Had my suggestion to see Brandy later in the week bruised her pride? After all, she and I are eerily similar it seems. Does *Kara* have someone else? Here? She turned up, somehow took over my life, and now, I'm pining for her. Strange how this resembles Cassie and her entry into my life. *Cassie. She had never wanted me.* Thinking of her doesn't bring the same agony and pain, so I'm clearly beginning to heal. What I said to Luc was true. Cassie had wreaked havoc wherever she went and in the end, it was that havoc that killed her. I hadn't failed her. But with Kara? *It had been bliss*, not havoc. Am I doomed to keep forming attachments to women who don't want me? I can't let myself turn Kara into some kind of twisted replacement for Cassie. I hate to even think that it could be a possibility, but I certainly allowed myself to develop feelings for her almost overnight, which never happens. It's always been Cassie in my heart and strangers who meant nothing in my bed. Even the ones I've seen on a more regular basis have never touched anything inside me other than lust. I certainly didn't spoon and cuddle. But with Kara, I'd done that and more. Part of her appeal is that she'd seemed just as lost as I was at times. She was a complex puzzle I wanted to solve, a soul I gravitated toward. And we were explosive in bed. Her cocky, sarcastic personality was so fucking sexy, and she took no prisoners. Shit, I really did miss the little smartass. I could use some comic relief right about now that's for sure. However, I'll let some time pass and put my focus where it needs to be. Then if the urge is still there, I'll find out where Kara is. After all, I have family connections, and I'm not afraid to use them.

CHAPTER SEVEN

Kara

I've descended into depression. Since Aidan left, I've regressed. I'm finally able to admit that to myself. For the first few days, I kept busy walking along the beach and shopping in town, but the nights were harder. I returned to the house Aidan had been renting every evening at the *normal* time. A part of me hoped his car would be there, but it never was. Then I'd return home and have several glasses of wine while I sat on my deck and watched the waves break onto the shore.

Uncle Lee calls to check on me a few times a week, as does my family. During one of his calls a few days after Aidan left, he told me Aidan's mother has cancer and that it isn't looking good. That effectively pushed me from feeling blue to crying for half the day. I wanted to pack my stuff, go home, and be there for the man I'd let myself care for. But then what? If there *was* any doubt he could handle my uncertain future, it is over now. There is no way he will want to become involved with someone whose cancer could return at any time. Statistically, it is highly probable the cancer will return as breast cancer sufferers under thirty-five are at very high risk.

He's texted me a few times, but I haven't heard anything from him in days. Since then, I've started to send him a message so many times, only to delete it. What is there to say? *Hey, I'm kind of crazy about you. PS . . . I might die of cancer at any moment.* Maybe I'm being melodramatic, but I can't see how he could want or need to get involved with me. If his mother passes away, that will be two people in just over one year he's loved and lost. How much could one man take? Cassie's death had driven him from his home for a long time, proving he was a man who felt deeply. He wouldn't just dust his hands off and move on to the next woman.

Decisions need to be made soon. When pressured to return home and resume my life, I have repeatedly given my parents a vague answer. I can't admit that some days I don't leave my bed. I know I'm spiraling out of control, but I'm just not sure I care. To my knowledge, no one has any idea that Aidan and I were involved while he was here. My family would have certainly mentioned that fact. I'd attempted to ask Uncle Lee a few questions when he'd imparted the awful news about Aidan's mom, but that's all he had known, and I couldn't dig deeper without rousing his curiosity.

I roll onto my side in the bed and clutch the pillow I'd taken from Aidan's house before I turned the key over to the owner. His scent is so vague that I have to bury my nose in the soft material to pick up a hint. Unfortunately, that sets off another crying episode, and between broken sobs, I vow to myself I won't let this continue. I'll cry out every last piece of Aidan Spencer tonight, and tomorrow, I'll make a plan. I've beaten cancer, for fuck's sake. Getting over a man who is little more than a stranger should be child's play. In the back of my mind, that irritating voice screams it won't be that easy, but I ignore it. Tonight, I need that shred of hope that I can forget how much he means to me and find myself again.

CHAPTER EIGHT

Aidan

To say the month I've been home has passed in a blur is an understatement. As I suspected, my mother is dying. She's stopped treatments and is content to spend her time with my father and me. Turns out, she knew the cancer had spread through her body and was just continuing chemo to buy some time until I came home. Talk about a bucket of fucking guilt. The day she revealed the truth to me, I'd wanted to rage at her. Instead, I walked out to lick my wounds before coming back and collapsing against her chest like a child.

I've also been angry with my father for lying to me about her prognosis when we talked the morning I'd come home. Once again, though, the buck stopped with me. My mother loved me so much that she'd been determined to give me time she didn't really have to give. She wanted me to heal, even if it cost her time with me. *How could she be so selfless when I'd been so selfish?* At the end, when my father knew time was getting short, he'd done something about it. A part of me still resents losing those precious months with her that I can never get back. When I mention that to her one night, she says that if I'd been here from the beginning, we would have wasted those extra months going to doctors. Now that part is over, and what we have left is the type of quality time we haven't spent together since I was a child. Every moment feels stolen and treasured.

We drove to the outer banks for a few days when she was feeling strong and wanted to smell the salty air one last time. When she's not felt as well, we've sat in the backyard and reminisced about the past. We've laughed more in this last month than I can ever remember. We're all adults now, and our bond is different than it was growing up. We're very much a family but also friends. Even though I'd remained close to my parents through the years, we'd never had the type of relationship we've developed this past month, and I regret it deeply. Again, I want to say if only there were more time. But I've come to accept that there will never be enough hours in the day or months on a calendar to say goodbye to someone who's helped shape me into the person I am today.

Luc has also been by to visit often. A few nights ago, he brought Lia and Lara over for dinner. My father cranked up the barbecue, and for a few hours, we all pretended that this was something we could do every month. Maybe start a new Sunday night tradition. I knew Luc was thinking exactly the same thing when I caught him staring at my mother with pain-filled eyes.

All too soon, the socializing came to a halt. Mom developed a cold that turned into pneumonia. Almost overnight, what little strength remained in her disease-ravaged body was zapped. No matter what they tried, nothing helped her bounce back, and I watched her grow weaker each day. She refused to be admitted to the hospital, so her doctor arranged for in-home hospice care. Even though a nurse was always in the house, my father and I took turns sitting with my mother, neither of us willing to give up precious time. We existed on a few hours of sleep and a whole lot of coffee.

She mostly sleeps, so I'm surprised when I feel her hand gripping mine as it rests on her bed. My eyes fly to hers, and I see her looking at me. She motions for me to remove her oxygen mask, and I get to my feet and gently lift it away. With an aching heart, I listen to her voice, scratchy from lack of use. "My baby boy."

She is so weak; it takes all I have to keep my shit together. "Hey, beautiful, it's good to see you awake. You're taking these naps way too far," I tease.

A shaky laugh escapes her chest, followed by a bout of coughing. I put the oxygen back on her until she's recovered and begins trying to remove it herself. "I hate that damn thing," she grumbles, surprising a laugh out of me. After being so out of it for the last week, she seems almost normal now, although a tad grumpy. I'm beginning to get my hopes up that perhaps she's turning a corner despite what her doctor says. Then she douses that like a bucket of water on a fire as she says, "Honey, I don't have much longer left with you." I open my mouth to protest, and she shushes me. "It's my time, baby, and I'm ready. My body is worn out, and I'm tired."

Shaking my head, I say, "That's just the pneumonia, Mom. When we get that under control, you'll feel better." It sounds irrational even to my ears, but I'm not ready to give up. *I'm not ready to say goodbye.*

"Aidan, I have cancer," she murmurs. "There is no getting better. I'm only going to continue to fade away every day, and I don't want to draw this out. I want you to remember me the way I've always been, not as some pathetic shell that lies in this bed for months on end until I waste away to nothing."

"But we don't have any way of knowing how much longer it will be," I argue. "You still have days ahead that will be better. Don't you want to stay for as long as you can?" I feel a tear roll down my cheek, and I flick it away impatiently. Her calm rationale is getting to me. It's as if she knows something the rest of us aren't privy to. *It has always been like this when I think about it.*

She shrugs her thin shoulder. "It's not my decision, son. But while I'm awake and have some of my thoughts together, I want to say some things, so please just humor your mother and listen to me ramble." I nod my head, knowing what's coming. I have no idea how I'll get through it, but I remain silent, giving her what she's asked for. She takes a deep breath and winces but begins speaking anyway. "I want you to know that I couldn't have asked for a better son than you, Aidan. You've been my pride and joy since the day you drew your first breath."

"Mom—don't," I manage to choke out past the huge lump in my throat.

"Sweet boy, let me finish," she chides. "You were a crazy and rambunctious boy who grew into an intelligent, driven, and thoughtful man. You're successful in business and have amazing friends who love you. Only one thing is missing from your life, and that's the type of love that you can only find with your soul mate."

Holy fucking shit, I can't believe she's going there. "Not everyone has that," I state calmly. "I tried, and it didn't happen. Sometimes, you have to realize that you weren't meant to go the traditional route."

"That's such a cop-out," she snaps.

"If you're trying to make this last speech warm and fuzzy, you're kind screwing it up," I point out wryly.

She giggles, which leads to yet another round of coughing before she gets herself back under control. "Let's face it, I've never been a traditional mom. I have too much personality for that. Plus, I always had to kick your butt when you were bad since your dad couldn't stand doing it."

"Please, neither could you." I laugh. "Both of you guys were always suckers for some tears."

Smirking, she says, "I knew half the time they weren't even real. But I figured if you went to the effort to rub water or spit on your face to fake a good cry, then you deserved to be cut some slack." She shifts around in bed, trying to get comfortable. "Now, as I was saying. I don't want you to close yourself off to finding love. I realize that you believe Cassie was the one for you, but that's not what I believe. I think if you break it down, you loved her in the same way you love Luc. But since she was a girl, and a beautiful one at that, your emotions just took over."

I really fucking hate talking about Cassie, especially to my mom. With anyone else, I'd end this right now, but shit, what am I supposed to do? This is my mother . . . who is dying. If this is the last real conversation we have, I can't possibly snap the way I want to. *Sit here and listen . . . for her. Let her die feeling as if she helped you.* "Mom, I think it was a bit more than that," I say gently, since she appears to be awaiting a response from me.

Her eyes are full of empathy as she stares into mine. "Maybe it was, son, but she wasn't the one for you. There was never any joy on your face or in your heart when she was around. You followed her around like a lost puppy, and she was more than happy to encourage that. In all the years you loved her, do you ever once recall being happy when she was near? Or were those moments always filled with torment? When you love someone, even if they're not yours, there should still be times you're together in simple ways that you treasure. Laughing over a joke. Remembering a smile over something silly. Countless moments captured in time that you play in your head like a movie when you're alone. Do you have any of that when you remember Cassie?"

Now I'm the one shifting on her bed as her words sink in, and I try to come up with even one instance I felt happy when I was with Cassie. And try as I might, every occasion had some type of turmoil involved. Dear God, had I never once just been glad to be with her? We were friends before she ended up with Luc. Shouldn't some kind of easy relationship have continued on, regardless of how I felt about her? *Fuck.* I drop my head and massage my temples. I don't want my mother to see how upset I am by this conversation. She's forced me to take my feelings out and examine them in a way that I've never done before, and it's shaken me to the core. "God," I hiss out, "I don't know what to think, Mom." And with those last words, I know I sound like her little boy again, lost and scared.

Obviously having heard it too, she motions me closer and runs her gaunt hand through my hair, soothing me as she always has. "Shhh, I didn't mean to hurt you, sweetheart. I just need you to see that *your* love is still out there. I couldn't leave you knowing you were so closed off to the future and what it holds for you. I want to look down on you and see you walking hand in hand with the woman you love. One who will make you laugh, smile, and even argue with passion. I want to see you with my grandchildren being the kind of man and father that I know you can be. Life is for living, my beautiful boy, not simply existing. The world is full of endless possibilities as long as you're open to letting them in."

"I hate this," I sob against her side as grief pierces my soul. She's saying goodbye to me in a way that only she can. "What joy can there possibly be in a future that doesn't include you?"

"But I'll be there, son," she assures me softly. "I'll be the hand on your shoulder when you need strength, the whispering wind on your face when you're sad, and the voice in your head urging you to reconsider when you're wrong. There is no power in this world great enough to keep me away from you. I may leave this broken body behind, but my spirit will never be far away. Whenever you need me, just close your eyes and I'll be there. Talk to me just as you are now. We may not have a relationship in the conventional sense, but the bonds we have will transcend even death. It's been a great honor and privilege to be your mother. Your father and I have done our very best to lead you down the right pathway in life. You're a man now, and I think you're ready to walk those same paths alone. Your father will be here for guidance and advice, and I'll be above for support. Just remember that even on your darkest days, I'll be a light for you to find your way."

"How can you promise me all of this?" I whisper, desperately wanting to believe in her slowly spoken, loving words. Not only are her words slicing apart my heart, but watching her wheeze and struggle to speak them is slaying me. *Such is the love of a mother, as they say.*

"Because after months of praying for answers, I finally found peace. Something that would have never happened had I not known in my heart that I'd be here for you in some form. I realize that it's difficult to accept, but I believe with everything inside me that I'll see you and your father live your lives. Hopefully, after I'm gone and you've had time to mourn, you'll discover the truth behind my words."

"I love you more than anything in this world," I say between sobs. My heart is shattering, and I can't imagine it ever coming back together again. How many times in your life can a heart break and heal itself? Despite her earlier assurances that I'll find love, it seems impossible in this instance. I fear I have nothing left to give to another.

"And I love you, my beautiful baby boy. Never, ever doubt that." She begins to tire, and her words are slurring. I lean over to drop a kiss on her cheek. I pull the oxygen mask back over her face and smooth her hair off her forehead. She's sleeping when I leave the room.

I rouse my dad from where he's dozing on the sofa. Since Mom is using their bedroom, he's set up camp in the living room. They have a couple spare bedrooms, but I don't think he can bring himself to use one of them. I wonder what he'll do when she's gone. Will any of us ever be able to stay in this house again without feeling her loss? On the other hand, I'm not sure my dad would be able to move for the same reason. He takes one look at my face and is on his feet. "We chatted for a while, so she's resting again now." *God, this is so hard.* "Go in. She'll know you're there." His eyes search mine as they always do when we "change shifts." We live each day now wondering if this will be her last. We both need that reassurance from the other that she's still fighting the fight. There is no way I can tell him about the conversation I had with her because he'd see it as a goodbye just as I did. And as crushing as it is to lose a mother, he's on the verge of losing a wife. The woman he made his life with. *His soul mate.* They've been together for almost forty years now. What it must be like to know you're going to lose that, and you can't do anything to stop it?

He's handled this better than I could have imagined. I've gained a newfound respect for his strength and courage. He's been determined to make her last days as peaceful for her as possible. While I've struggled with depression, he's soldiered on, carrying not only my mother at times but me as well. Truthfully, I don't think I could have held it together without him. I've always thought of my father as an exceptional man, but I've also been privileged to see why my mother loves him so much. He's the rock that supported her and the safety net there to catch her. She was able to shine like the brightest star because she never had to fear losing her way. He was her true north and that hasn't changed. *Will I ever be that to a woman? Do I have that in me?* I squeeze his shoulder as he moves toward the door. "She's talking today?"

"Yeah, she is." I smile. "She made me take the oxygen mask off. At one point, there was even some profanity," I joke, trying to lighten the mood.

He looks somewhat calmer now that I feel like I'm sending a lamb to the slaughter. We've both harbored hope that she'd have some miracle recovery, but I know now. *That* isn't going to happen. She's leaving us, and it's going to happen soon. It's not my place to tell him that, though. *He'll know soon enough.* My mother is saying her goodbyes, and he's almost certainly next in line to receive his. I have a feeling his strength will be tested, and his walls will crumble. At some point, losing a loved one must be faced, and there is no way for anyone to make that better. You can only hope that somewhere down the line you'll be able to pick up the pieces left behind and face the day without giving in to the sorrow within. Somehow, you learn to live with the hole in your heart created by their death. *Somehow.*

CHAPTER NINE

Kara

I sit in the back pew of the church while the pastor delivers the eulogy for Ginny Spencer. I fought a battle with myself when Uncle Lee told me about Aidan's mom passing away. But in the end, I was almost obsessed with attending her funeral. Why, I don't know. Aidan isn't even aware I'm here. I sent flowers, but the odds of him actually knowing that with the amount of them decorating the church is small.

The room is so crowded that I've been able to do little but make out the back of his head. Lucian, followed by other friends and family, has given his speech. Neither Aidan nor his father spoke, which is understandable. I'm sure they're barely holding it together. I know from the times he talked about his parents that they were extremely close, and he is an only child.

When the moment arrives for the family to leave the church for the graveside service, I brace to see Aidan make his exit. Instead, he walks to the coffin and takes up a position on the side, as does his father. Then Lucian takes the lead, along with Max Denton and a couple of other men I don't recognize. As the casket makes its way through the church and up the aisle, I watch the man who has come to mean so much to me. His face is noticeably thinner, and his eyes are red rimmed and glassy. He's cut his hair, which only seems to emphasize the paleness of his features.

I am so busy drinking in every detail of him that when I reach his eyes once again, I'm startled to see him staring back at me. His face floods with recognition and for a brief moment, time stands still, and there is only the two of us. My lips part and my insides quiver. God, I've missed him so much it hurts. *"Aidan."* His name is a whisper on my lips, and I know he sees it. Then almost in the blink of an eye, it's over, and he's passing the bench where I'm sitting. I feel boneless as I slump back against the bench. If that had been a test to see if my heart had let him go, I'd just failed. Just seeing him again literally makes my heart hurt. He is clearly in so much pain, and I want nothing more than to put my arms around him and soothe the hurt.

My mother and father are out of town on a long overdue holiday, but Uncle Lee is sitting several rows ahead of me. I'm sure he'll be surprised to see me here since he doesn't know about my association with Aidan. I get to my feet when everyone else does, prepared to go to my car and skip the graveside service. I've made it a few steps when I feel a hand on my arm. Whirling around in surprise, I see Lia standing there with a smile on her face. "Kara, I thought that was you. Lee didn't tell me you were home."

I give her a hug, genuinely happy to see her. Thanks to my cancer and recovery, I have spent very little time with the newest addition to the Jacks family, which is something I regret. I know she had a tough life growing up with an abusive mother and stepfather. My uncle was crushed when he found out he had a daughter in her twenties he'd never known about. He stepped up immediately and has built a strong relationship with her. Truthfully, I've never seen him happier. "I just got home yesterday, so I don't think he even knows. Where's Lara?" I ask, looking around for Lia's fourteen-month-old daughter. A wave of guilt hits me as I realize I barely know her either. My cancer was so much more than an illness. It took away my interest in life and everyone in it. I'm so tired of being that person. I never understood how it was to be in a room full of people yet feel so completely alone as I do right now. Even as I smile and make polite conversation with her, a big part of me is removed from what's going on. I'm on autopilot as usual, and I fucking hate it. I want to be myself again. This robot I've let myself become isn't me.

"She's with our nanny. I didn't want her to be a disruption during the service today, and she's not very good at staying still or quiet for long. Hey, do you want to ride to the other service with me? Luc's going to be in the family car with Aidan." It's on the tip of my tongue to refuse, but minutes later, I'm sitting next to a cousin I barely know. *How I yearn for that to change. I want Lia in my life.*

It's just a few miles to the cemetery, and all too soon, I'm on Lia's other side while she stands next to Aidan. His head is down as the pastor speaks, and I see his shoulders shake. Luc is standing between who I assume is Aidan's father and Aidan trying to comfort them as best he can. I have no idea how it happens, but when I hear a sob escape from his lips, I move, almost as if unaware of what I'm doing. I care deeply for this man, and he's hurting. I give no thought to the fact that he may not even want me here. The bond formed between us in those weeks we had together simply will not let me turn away from his pain. I nudge Lia aside and touch his hand. He looks down at me, and I see such staggering anguish there, I slide my arm around him and lay my head on his shoulder. He stiffens for a moment and then collapses against me. His head drops to the top of mine, and we're clinging to each other. I've no doubt that we've drawn attention, especially from our immediate group of friends and family, but I could give a shit. He needs me now, and that's all that matters.

I barely recall meeting Aidan's parents at Luc's wedding, but I'm crying for the loss of a woman so obviously loved. *I'm crying for the loss this man beside me is enduring. Life simply isn't fair sometimes.* As the service ends, he takes a couple of deep breaths as he fights to get himself under control. *Why should he? He's just lost his mom, so why should he have to be under control? He should be allowed to grieve, to sob in his loss.* I rub my hand soothingly up and down his back, and his grip on me tightens for a moment before relaxing. He's gathered his composure now, and he gently pulls away from my embrace. When my arms fall to my side, he reaches down and takes one of my hands in his. No words pass between us, which should be strange but somehow isn't. He shakes hands with what seems like hundreds of people as he accepts their words of condolence. Luc says something to him about going back to the house for a gathering, but Aidan shakes his head. He turns to Lia who is still next to me and asks, "Did you drive here?" When she nods, he asks, "Can I borrow your car? I need to get away for a while."

"Of course, I'll go with Luc," she says softly as she hands him her keys. I think he'll let me go at this point, but he keeps a firm hold as he stops to whisper something to his father, and then we're walking away from the remaining crowd and toward the parking lot.

He flips a button to unlock the car and then opens the passenger door for me. I look up at him, but his expression is blank and impassive. The emotion from earlier is gone, and I can almost believe I imagined it except for the redness remaining around his beautiful eyes. I stand for a moment uncertain of what I'm doing here until he crushes all of my indecision with a few quietly spoken words. "I need you, princess." That's it. I'm done for. I settle into the leather seat, and he shuts the door behind me. He walks around the front of the car and gets in the driver's side.

"Where are we going?" I ask when it's obvious he doesn't intend to fill the silence.

He shrugs. "To my place. Everyone is going back to my parents'—my dad's house—and I just need some distance for now."

I reach over and put my hand on his arm. "I'm so sorry about your mom." It seems pointless to add any false sentiment since I didn't know her. I also have a feeling he's heard as much of that as he can handle for the day.

He nods his head once to acknowledge my words before saying, "I was so damn surprised to see you in the church. How long have you been back?"

I think about lying, not sure how it'll sound if I admit that I only came back to be here for him. *Screw it.* "I got in last night. Uncle Lee told me about your mom, and I wanted to come today."

He shocks me when he admits, "I've missed you, princess. I came back home to one of my worst nightmares, and it's pretty damned ironic when I thought I'd already lived through that. Some days when Mom was sleeping, and I had a minute to myself, I thought about you. Wondered if you were still at the beach or if you'd moved on to somewhere else. I wanted to call just to hear your voice, but I didn't think you'd answer your phone."

I swallow the lump in my throat because he's undoubtedly right. Even though I ached to be with him again, I'd spent weeks after he left trying to convince myself it could never happen. Hell, I shouldn't be here now. The last thing he needs after losing his mother is comfort from a woman who is barely holding it together most days. *What could I offer him?* I knew he'd been through hell; it was there on his face. At the very least, I was high risk and always would be. And I felt like an imposter sitting beside him as if I had more to offer than I did.

Soon, we are pulling into the underground parking garage below some upscale condominiums. He parks in a spot near the elevator and gets out. Before I can find the door handle, he has it open and a hand on my arm to help me out. He closes the door and puts a hand on the small of my back, directing me forward to the elevator. Once inside, he presses the button for the tenth floor and settles back against the dark paneling of the compartment. The quiet is becoming unnerving, but I don't attempt to break it. Naturally, he isn't in the mood for chitchat after the day he's had.

We walk to the end of the hallway, and I see a door hidden away in a small alcove. He removes a key from his pocket, opens it, and then motions me forward. His home is modern with neutral colors, but the overstuffed furniture looks surprisingly worn and comfortable. This isn't just a show place. Aidan lives and relaxes here. It also makes me wonder how many women he's brought here, but I tamp down the jealousy that streaks through me. We're not in a relationship, and I have no right to feel territorial. He tosses his keys and wallet on the granite bar area of the kitchen before walking over to a bar and picking up a bottle. He raises it in the air and says, "No need to dirty a glass. Want to join me, princess?"

"Whatever you need," I say softly, expecting him to take it to the sofa. Instead, he lowers himself to the floor and puts his back against the wall before unscrewing the cap and taking a long drink. His eyes are on me as if waiting to see what I'll do. Finally, I kick off my high heels and cross to him. I kneel down, take the bottle from his hands, and put it to my lips. The first sip burns like fire down my throat, and I wheeze, wondering what in the hell he's drinking. He thumps me on the back as he chuckles. Then he pulls me down next to him, and we pass the bottle back and forth. It isn't long before my head is spinning and we're both giggling over absolutely nothing. Then something changes; I look over and ache at the tears I see running down his face. His laughter has turned to sobbing as the alcohol breaks his control. I crawl unsteadily over to him and get in his lap, wrapping my legs around him. I take his head in my hands kissing the trail of wetness streaking his cheeks.

I have no idea how long we stay that way. At some point, I put my arms around his shoulders, and we lay our heads side by side. "Kara." He sighs against me as a giant shudder wracks his body.

"I'm here, baby," I whisper, turning to kiss his neck. Then as if in slow motion, our clothes are off. How we manage that, I can't say, but he's pulling me back over his lap and impaling me on his hard cock. He's not wearing a condom, and I can feel the difference immediately, but I let it go. I'm on birth control, and we had the discussion at one point about recent STD testing. I know Aidan would never lie to me about that. Our mating begins at a frantic pace but soon slows to a leisurely fucking that threatens to overwhelm my heart and body. Our lips cling to each other as our tongues glide wetly together. *I've missed this. Him.* He's devouring me as if starved for my taste, and I'm right there with him. Our hands are moving, constantly touching and rediscovering. With each stroke of his fingertips, he leaves liquid fire behind.

"You. Feel. So. Fucking. Good." Somehow, the pause between each word makes his statement that much hotter. "I want everything you've got, princess. I'm going to own you, body and soul." He thrusts his hips upward, pushing his cock to brush against my cervix. I wince at the brief stab of discomfort before the pleasure comes flooding back. Aidan Spencer has a big cock, and God, does he know how to work it. He pulls back slightly and lowers his hand between us, finding my clit easily. He rubs it firmly, and I see stars. I cry out in protest when his fingers move away to cover my pussy. "I own this, do you hear me? It's fucking *mine.*" I nod my head because I would pretty much agree to anything at this moment with my orgasm so very close to the surface. He clucks his tongue before demanding, "Say the words, princess." He's stopped moving, and his cock is at a standstill buried deep inside me.

"What do you want?" I cry out. I attempt to move my hips and gain the friction I need, but one hand locks me in place. "Aidan . . ." I whimper, trying to figure out why he's denying us both.

"Say you're mine," he hisses as I fidget against him. "Give me the words. I just—need them today."

Even though alarm bells are going off in my head and I know it's wrong to pretend this is anything other than sex, I do as he asks. Hell, I'm not really lying. At this moment, I've never belonged to another man as much as I do him. So I give him what he wants. Lowering my mouth to his ear, I whisper, "I'm yours. I don't want anyone but you." He throws his head back, groaning my name, and then he's fucking me hard. I can only grab his shoulders and hold on as he lifts me almost completely off his cock before slamming me back down. "Aidan! Oh, my God!" I'm screaming his name over and over as I come. My orgasm seems to have no end as I continue to spasm around his still-pumping cock. I'd have long since fallen over if not for his firm grip on me. I've no doubt I'll be bruised and sore from this rough possession, but Aidan isn't getting away without being marked either. My nails have scored gashes on his back and arms, and I've bitten his shoulders and neck countless times as if trying to consume him.

Finally, when I'm so lightheaded and limp that I'm not sure I can take any more pleasure, I feel his warm seed shoot deep inside me and he yells my name on a hoarse shout.

"Every time, princess. So good," he says quietly.

I expect him to pull away after that. To want some distance between us. Aidan was charmingly affectionate in our time together, but I wouldn't really call it intimate, but for possibly a few occasions. Today is different, though. I wince a bit as he pulls his cock from me, and I feel the moisture begin to trickle out. He pulls me tighter and somehow finds his feet while balancing my weight against him. He walks through his home until we reach the bathroom. Still holding me, he sticks a hand into the oversize shower in the corner, turns both knobs, and then steps inside. Only then does he gently put me on my feet, while luckily keeping an arm around me until I'm steady. His eyes are hooded as he washes himself and then turns to do the same with me. It's as if his mind is a million miles away, no doubt processing the last few days. Maybe my arrival too. There's nothing sexual in his touch now; he's focused on the task at hand and does it with brisk efficiency. I yearn to know how I can best care for him, yet at this moment, he *needs* to look after me. When we're both clean to his satisfaction, he steps out and grabs a couple of towels from a nearby closet, wrapping one around his hips. He helps me out and carefully enfolds me in the other one, kissing me on the forehead as he does. "Come on, beautiful, let's get you dry and then we'll have a bite to eat."

He has me sit on the large vanity and dries my hair. I don't know what to make of this Aidan, who seems intent on catering to my every need. Maybe he needs this busywork right now to take his mind off his loss. With that in mind, I don't voice any objections as he leads me to the bedroom next and into a huge walk-in closet where he locates a T-shirt for me. He quickly dresses in a pair of basketball shorts and another T-shirt, and then we're heading back toward the kitchen. "Why don't you have a seat and I'll make something for us?" I offer. I expect him to argue, but surprisingly, he goes to a barstool without complaint. *It's been five weeks, but preparing food for him in his kitchen feels normal.* I pad around his luxury kitchen and take a moment to appreciate the array of granite and stainless steel. I wonder if he cooks a lot because he certainly has the best of everything here. I quickly wash my hands before I sift through the cabinets and come up with a box of spaghetti and a jar of gourmet marinara sauce. Perfect. Quick and easy. I put a pot of water on to boil and open the jar. I put the tip of my finger in and then stick it in my mouth. Bold flavors explode on my tongue, and I moan my approval.

I startle when Aidan says, "You're killing me over here, princess. If you don't get that finger out of your mouth, you'll be sucking something else pretty soon." His eyes are on fire when I look over at him, and I wonder how in the world he can want me again after just fucking me minutes ago. But I've learned that Aidan needs little to no recovery time, and he's certainly never had a problem with admitting how much he desires me. I giggle and stick my tongue out at him before finding another pot for the sauce and dumping it in. He clears his throat then surprises me by saying, "Thanks for being here today, babe. You've no idea how much I needed it—and you."

My throat tightens, and my eyes water as his words wrap around me and squeeze my heart. This is a different Aidan than I knew before. He's quieter, but somehow even more intense. Losing his mother has changed something fundamentally inside him, and I'm not sure what to make of it. "You're . . . welcome," I manage to stutter out. Then for some reason, I keep talking even though I try to tell myself to stop. "I wasn't sure if I should come or not. I mean I know that what we had was like a beach fling or whatever the cool people are calling it these days, but we're connected through our families so that makes us friends as well—I think. But I don't want you to feel as if I'm stalking you or anything. I didn't expect to pick up where we left off when I came back, so if you're afraid of that, then don't worry." He gets off his stool and walks toward me. Actually, it's more like stalking. He looks amused and something else I can't define. And dear God, the verbal diarrhea just continues to dribble from my mouth. "Or I could just go right now. Wait, I'll finish making you dinner since I said I would, but you must be ready to relax, and you probably don't want to entertain." I laugh, and it sounds horribly shrill and nervous as I add, "I don't want to be that guest who came and didn't know when to leave. No one wants to be—"

His fingers clamp down on my lips, and weird shrieks escape as I still attempt to talk around them. "Baby—shut the fuck up." He chuckles. "Do you realize that you haven't taken a breath in at least two minutes?" He releases my mouth and gently moves me to the side so he can add the spaghetti to the now boiling water. Then he's back, and his hands are on my hips. "Now, let's get a couple of things straight, princess. I'm not your buddy or your friend. Truthfully, I don't know what the hell I am. But I don't want to fuck my friends or family so that means you're neither. I want you here with me so don't even think about leaving. We don't need to have all the answers tonight or make this into something complicated." He takes my face in his hands and drops a kiss on my mouth. "I just want to spend some time—with you. Let's take it as it comes and see where we go. No running, no freaking out. Just two people enjoying each other. Can you do that, princess?"

Even as I tell myself to make up some excuse and leave, I find my traitorous mouth murmuring, "Yeah, I can do that."

And that's the moment that I'll look back on. That one fleeting instance when I could have done the right thing, but I let my heart lead me astray. I convinced myself that he needed me for a little longer. Hadn't he lost his mother? Weren't friends supposed to be there for you no matter the cost? Yeah, I sold myself on every one of those sentimental pieces of drivel. And it would all come back to haunt me when the truth came out. But I couldn't stop.

It was already too late for me.

I'd fallen for a man I barely knew, and the clock had been ticking down the time we had together since before our first kiss.

Aidan

I can hardly believe Kara is here and sleeping soundly in my bed. Making my way up the aisle in the church carrying my mother's body in that fucking cold metal box, I'd been as close to losing my shit in public as I'd ever been. I'd been seriously afraid I was going to have some kind of panic attack right there. My eyes had flittered around me, desperately seeking a diversion. At first, I had passed right over her. My mind sluggish and my thoughts scattered. Then something had penetrated the fog that surrounded me, and I'd turned my head, seeking her out once again. And there she stood staring at me in a rare, unguarded moment. Her eyes had been full of pain and emotion. She'll never know how much it meant to me that she was there. Her very presence calmed and leveled me enough that I was able to carry on. I kept telling myself to just get through the rest of the service, and then I could find her and escape. And that's exactly what I'd done.

The night closes in around me as I think again about the last moments with my mother. She had died two days after our talk. I'd known in my heart that it was her final goodbye, even though other than her difficulty breathing, she'd seemed just like her old self. Somehow, she'd managed to conserve her strength for God knows how long to have that time with my father and me. I'd been on autopilot ever since. Arrangements were made and finalized. Friends and coworkers were in and out, and I said all the right things. I even joked around when inside I wanted to tell them to get the fuck out. Only Luc seemed to know what was simmering right below the surface. I could feel his understanding empathy. That much penetrated the protective haze I was hiding behind. He'd dealt with enough trauma in his life to understand that sometimes you just had to shut down or else you'd lose it.

Dad was doing better than I would have expected. Although, I'm sure it's hitting him about now that she's never coming back. When someone dies, there's so little time to dwell on your loss because you're mired down in the details. Behind everything in life, there's a business, and death is no exception. Services are rendered, and people have to be paid. I'd wager that the toughest time grieving people face is the week after the funeral. Then you're finally alone, and there's nothing left to do. People have moved on with their lives, and you're left in an empty house with some leftover cake and a fuck load of memories. *And very alone.*

I'm not sure that death is ever easy. Everyone assumes that they'll live to a ripe old age. When your grandparents die, it's upsetting, but you kind of expect it. What you don't plan on is the suddenness with which someone you love can be wrenched from this world. Cassie's death happened so quickly that it was over before I could even process it. I spent a year trying to figure out exactly what the fuck went wrong. It was senseless and downright horrifying. It was also an eye-opening look into how fleeting life can be. Before that, even with her living in a mental institution, I still thought I had all the time in the world to make things better. Yeah, not so fucking fast, said the universe. Want to know how small and insignificant you are in the scheme of things? Try to save someone you love.

I liken someone attempting to beat cancer to pissing in the wind. All my efforts appeared to serve no purpose and to be absolutely pointless. Again, the grim reaper was just around the corner, and he doesn't fucking fight fair. Hell, the battle was over before I even knew it had started. I guess I should be grateful that I had a few stolen moments in both instances that I'll carry with me forever before they were gone. I'd been angry with God and the world when Cassie died. With my mom, I feel nothing but overwhelming sorrow. I never imagined a life without either one of my parents. They'd always seemed ageless to me. There's also a healthy dose of guilt for the fact that I basically cut them out of my life for a year, and they loved me enough to give me that, even when she was sick. I want those days, weeks, and months back. What I wouldn't give to walk in the door of my childhood home in the morning and hear her calling out to me. As their only son, I feel as if I've failed them both. And even though it's too late to make it up to her, I vow that I will honor her wish of watching out for my father. It's the only thing I can remember her ever truly asking of me. Plus, I'm pretty damn sure her promise of watching us from above is true. If anyone can manage that, it will be my mother. Heaven doesn't know what's in store for with Ginny Spencer in residence now.

Kara mumbles something under her breath and burrows deeper under the covers. The moonlight shining in from the window makes her look like an angel. Her arms are wrapped around one of my pillows, and she's snoring delicately. It amazes me how much I've come to care about her in such a short amount of time. The weeks apart hasn't changed that. If anything, I feel closer to her now. There's been a shift in our relationship, and I can pinpoint the exact moment when I knew she felt it too. In the kitchen earlier when she'd been rattling on, and I'd said that I wanted to spend time with her and asked if she could give me that. Her first instinct had been to run. It was written all over her face. Hell, I'd even braced for the rejection. But she'd fought past whatever was holding her back and had agreed. After that, the tension had left her body, and for the first time since we met, she'd given me all of herself for the rest of the evening. I had no idea what would happen when we woke in the morning, but I'll cross that bridge when I had to. The one thing I do know is that I plan to see where things go with her. I'd promised my mother not to close myself off, and since Kara is the only woman other than

Cassie to ever make me feel, I can't ignore the possibility of something there worth pursuing.

With my mind now as tired as my body, I relax back into the bed and pull her into my arms. She wraps herself around me as if she'd been doing it for years, and I feel at peace for the first time in weeks as I drift away, lulled by the sound of her heart beating against mine.

CHAPTER TEN

Kara

I'd argued, but Aidan insisted on dropping me off at my parents' house. My mother had called that morning to let me know they'd arrived home during the night and were eager to see me. Pretty sure that translated into, "Someone told us you were all over Aidan Spencer at his mother's funeral." When he pulls into the circular drive and puts the car in park, I unbuckle my seat belt. "Thanks for the ride," I say lightly with one hand already on the door handle.

He reaches out and grips my arm. "Let me walk you in. I don't want your parents to think I just dumped you and took off."

I laugh, hoping it doesn't sound as forced as it feels. There is no way I want him running into my parents. I don't want them accidentally blurting something out, even though there's no reason they would. You have to worry about that kind of stuff when you're living a lie, though. Little things tripping you up. "We're not in high school, babe. You don't have to shake my father's hand and promise him that you didn't go past first base last night." Wiggling my brows, I add, "Because we both know you hit a homer to right field and slid into the plate."

He throws back his head and chuckles. God, I love this Aidan. He's so flipping sexy like this. I feel ridiculously pleased with myself that I'm the one who's managed to chase some of the shadows from those beautiful blue eyes. I can't stand the thought of them returning, as they inevitably will. After all, he just buried his mother yesterday. He's a long way from carefree. "I like the dirty baseball references, princess. They make my dick hard." Shaking his head, he murmurs, "Of course, just being in the same zip code with you makes me that way."

I put my hand over his zipper and feel the truth in his words. "You've certainly got a problem there, slugger. Maybe we can get in some batting practice later. You know—help you improve that swing and all." I giggle at his indignant expression. Men and their fragile egos. One word about their performance and they're sulking.

I have my door open, and I'm giving him my best angelic smile when he says, "You'd better take it easy today, sweetheart. Tonight, I'll hit a fastball right down the centerline. I can't be responsible for what happens if you fail to field it." My knees squeeze together as his words have their desired effect on me. Naturally, he doesn't miss it, and I swear his ego is so damn big I'm surprised it fits in the car. "If you're a good girl, princess, I'll take care of that for you later on. Now close the door and your mouth so I can leave. Otherwise, I'm walking you to the door and telling your daddy what a bad girl you've been."

I slam the door so hard the car rocks. Then I move quickly down the walkway and ring the doorbell since I don't have my house key with me. A quick glance over my shoulder has me sagging in relief when I see Aidan pulling back out onto the main road. I swear the bastard loves to see me squirm. I can only imagine how uncomfortable he may feel spending just five minutes with my parents. Tons of double-entendre might fly over my mother's head but would likely register with my father eventually. He prides himself on maintaining his street lingo for some reason. I know that he and my uncle Lee basically raised themselves and lived a life that he'll never fully reveal to his children. I don't know if my mother even knows the whole story. I've heard enough rumors to know that my uncle is a powerful man on both sides of the law. There's no way I'd be working for him now, though, if my father thought for a minute anything illegal was happening at Falco Industries.

My father opens the door with a frown on his face. "Hey, baby, why're you ringing the bell? Last time I checked, you still lived here."

"Hey, Daddy." I smile before throwing myself into his muscular arms. I'm close to both of my parents, but my father and I share so many similar traits that we can often finish each other's sentences. There has always been a special bond between us, and I'm so thankful for him. I've had him wrapped around my finger from the moment I knew it was possible, and that's never changed.

He enfolds me in a strong embrace, nearly squeezing the breath out of me. "God, I've missed my girl so much." He sighs against the top of my hair. When I pull back, he studies my face as if looking for answers before he asks the first questions. "How've you been, baby? I was on the verge of begging your uncle to evict you so you'd come home. You know how your mother worries." I bite back a smile because we both know my father is the one who stresses over his family.

"I'm doing great, Daddy," I assure him. "It's good to be home, though. Where are Mom and Kyle?"

"Your brother is on some trip with his fraternity." Cringing, he adds, "The less I know about that, the better. When he needs bail money, I'm sure I'll hear from him. And your mom is in the kitchen having coffee. I'll go ahead and warn you that one of her friends told her about you and Aidan Spencer being *affectionate* toward each other. She barely slept a wink last night. What's going on there—"

"Pete, who was at the door?" my mother calls from the other room.

My dad shakes his head ruefully and motions me forward. "I swear it's like she knows," he whispers as we make our way down the hall and into the bright and airy kitchen at the end of it. My mother is sitting at the kitchen table wearing her reading glasses while she flips through the morning paper. She's a gorgeous woman who has maintained her slim build and has beautiful, long blond hair. She could easily pass for someone years younger than her forty-five. I've always been so proud to have such a beautiful mom. Other kids were embarrassed when their moms dropped by school, but I was the exact opposite.

Her face lights up when she sees me in the doorway. She gets to her feet and crosses the room at a near run. I'm once again hugged tightly. "Oh sweetheart, there you are. Your father has been just beside himself since you've been gone. I could barely keep him from going after you." I turn my head sideways and smirk at my dad. He gives me a sheepish grin as if to acknowledge that he's been busted but couldn't care less. She takes my hand and pulls me toward the table. "Come sit down and tell us what you've been up to. Did you make any new friends while you were away?"

My father winks at me as he takes a seat next to my mother. We both know she's dying to ask about Aidan but is hoping I'll just volunteer the information. "I had a nice, relaxing vacation at the beach. I did a lot of walking and swimming. I made a few friends there. The bartender at the outdoor bar was awesome. We're officially Facebook friends now, and I'm following him on Twitter. It's too soon for Instagram, but I can't rule it out." I bite my lip to keep from laughing at my mother's bemused expression. My dad is looking everywhere but at us, trying to keep his smile under control as well. We both know I'm screwing with her, but she still hasn't put it together yet.

"Er . . . I'm sure he's a perfectly nice man. But what about Aidan Spencer?" she finally blurts out. "Catherine Sullivan said you were all up on him at his mother's funeral yesterday."

All up on him? I mouth to my father as he looks away with his shoulders shaking. Oh, dear Lord, my mother must be watching reality television again. When she was addicted to *Jersey Shore,* it was impossible to have a conversation with her that didn't include some type of slang. She's a member of two county clubs, for heaven's sake. How have those blue bloods not shamed her out of that habit by now? "Aidan is a . . . friend of mine," I finally say. "I was helping him through a difficult situation."

This time, my father cuts in with, "But how do you even know him? I mean you've probably met in passing somewhere along the line, but that's it, right?"

"Well, that's actually an interesting story," I say brightly. "Turns out he was also staying in Charleston while I was there. We met one night at the outdoor bar and recognized each other."

My mother wrinkles her nose, looking perplexed as she asks, "So you what—became friends?"

Boy, what a tough crowd. Their eyes focus on me as if waiting for my answer anxiously. "Um . . . kind of," I say evasively. "We had dinner together some evenings and hung out on the beach."

Showing no sign of lightening up on the rapid-fire questions, my mom asks, "Is he your boyfriend now?" Then she makes quotation marks with her fingers and adds, "Or is this a casual hook up? I mean, if you were that close at the funeral, there must be a little more going on here than friends. From what I remember, he's quite the hunk." My father clears his throat as if voicing his objection of her description, and she pats him on the hand. "Oh relax, babe, I'm just giving Kara some support."

I get to my feet and grab a cup out of a nearby cabinet then pour myself some coffee. After a few sips, I settle back in my seat before admitting, "I don't really know what Aidan is. We were kind of seeing each other in Charleston, but then he found out about his mom and had to come back. We didn't stay in touch after that. That is partly my fault because he did text me a few times. Then Uncle Lee told me about his mother passing away, and I don't know . . . I felt like I needed to be here." Although I'm not planning to share every detail with my parents, it is actually really good to talk to someone about Aidan. During our weeks together, but especially during our weeks apart, I didn't tell anyone. I don't have many close girlfriends anymore, so speaking about him is in some ways cathartic. Necessary. A . . . relief.

"You could do worse," my mom adds helpfully. "From what I've gathered from your father and Google, he's a very successful man. He's the best friend and right hand of Lucian Quinn."

Exasperated, I say, "Mom, I know who Lucian is. After all, my cousin is married to him. And why in the world would you be googling Aidan? Isn't that some kind of invasion of privacy?"

"Not if he doesn't know about it," she argues. "Plus, you're my only daughter. It's my job to make sure you're not dating some kind of pervert or convict. Did you know that almost all states have their criminal records online now? For a small fee, a parent can really have some peace of mind."

I drop my head onto the table, barely resisting the urge to bang it a few times for good measure. Why in the world did my father ever buy her a computer? I swear the woman can tell you the address of every sex offender in the state. Now, she's adding Aidan to her usual round of nosy detective work. Knowing him, he'll be amused, but I don't want to risk finding out. "Dad," I mumble without raising my head, "can you please pull the plug on her Wi-Fi access?" He chuckles, and I'm afraid I hear them kissing like teenagers. I stay where I am for a few moments longer to miss their usual PDA before lifting my head and frowning at their flushed expressions. As much as I grumble about it, I love the fact that my parents are still so crazy about each other.

"Sorry, baby," my dad says not looking in the least repentant. "You know your mother is a free spirit. Just be glad that I draw the line at letting her break into Aidan's house or lift his fingerprints."

"You can actually do that now, you know," my mother pipes in. "Have someone use a glass and then mail it to this company that charges fifty dollars to run them through their nationwide system."

My father and I both groan at the same time. "That's great to know, Mom, I'll keep that in mind," I say sarcastically. I'm surprised I ever had a date growing up. Luckily, she's able to keep some of her crazy under wraps when there are guests present.

Then comes the inevitable question that I always hate because it's no longer just an innocent inquiry into my well-being. "So, honey, how have you been feeling?" my mom asks, looking me up and down as if hunting for defective parts.

"I'm good, Mom. Well rested from my vacation and ready to get back to work for Uncle Lee."

"You remember you have an appointment with your oncologist in a few weeks, right?" my dad asks quietly. The mood in the kitchen is so damn somber now. Mentioning the dreaded cancer takes us all back to those days of chemo and surgery. Another thing I hate about this fucking disease is that we'll never be a normal family again. It's always there below the surface. The dread, the worry, the uncertainty.

Keeping my face carefully blank, I nod my head. "I know. I set a reminder on my phone. It's routine, though, so there's no need to worry you guys."

My mom's hands tremble on her cup as she asks, "You're still doing your breast exams, right? Early detection is so important. I wish you'd had the double mastectomy. Why didn't—"

"Mom," I say sternly. "The doctor said it wasn't necessary, and the cancer can come back somewhere else."

"We're not trying to upset you," my dad says quietly. "We worry, that's all."

My shoulders droop, and I feel like an ungrateful bitch. I have a wonderfully, supportive family and lashing out at them is the last thing I should be doing. "I know, and I'm sorry." I attempt a smile. "It would be great if we could all go back to the days when that wasn't necessary, but we can't. I promise I'm doing my self-exams, and if anything out of the ordinary comes up, I'll call the doctor right away."

My father, bless his heart, changes the subject for which I'm grateful. "So when are you coming back to Falco?"

My mother grabs his arm, saying excitedly, "Have you told Kara about Liza?"

My father rolls his eyes. "No, honey, this is the first time I've seen her as well. And we probably shouldn't be gossiping about it. Lee hasn't told us anything concrete."

I sit up straighter, sensing a good story here. Liza has been Uncle Lee's assistant for several years, and I absolutely adore her. She's sweet but knows how to kick ass when need be. She's also absolutely gorgeous and single. I've often wondered why my uncle doesn't seem to notice those facts. "All right, well, someone is damn well going to talk now. You can't leave me hanging like this."

"Language, Kara." My father clicks his tongue. *Thank goodness my father hasn't heard Aidan speak when we're alone. Not that I mind . . .*

My mother leans forward in her seat and drops her voice to a whisper for some strange reason. "Liza quit. She handed in her notice during a meeting. She called Lee a blind fool and said she wasn't going to waste her whole life waiting on him. Apparently, he's been frantic to get her back, but she's not taking his calls. She's also not staying at home because he's been going by there trying to see her."

I know my eyes are huge as I say, "Wow. I can't believe Liza quit. She loves working at Falco. And what is Uncle Lee doing without her? She handled everything for him. I bet he's chasing his ass all day long now." When I see my father's scowl, I realize I've let another curse word out. It's hard to believe a man raised on the streets is so particular about that. "Sorry, Dad," I toss in, and he winks.

"It's been tough on Lee," my father admits. "We've already gone through a string of temps, but he keeps finding fault with them. The office is a mess right now. No one stays long enough to get anything done. I've been spending my day answering the phones, if you can believe it." He gives me a hopeful look. "Maybe you can take over for a while until we figure something out. At least Lee isn't likely to fire you."

"Of course, I will," I readily agree. "Although don't expect a miracle. I have no idea how Liza managed to run everything so seamlessly. I can answer the phones while I attempt to figure it out. In the meantime, he needs to step up his efforts to find her and grovel. He must have been a jerk for her to quit."

"He claims he doesn't know what caused it," my dad says, not sounding convinced.

"Oh, he knows all right," my mom murmurs. "Liza has been in love with that man for years. You'd have to be blind not to see it. She's basically been the woman in his life, with none of the perks that come along with it." Turning to Dad, she says, "Remember how excited she was when he asked her to accompany him to that charity ball last year? They made such a striking couple. I know she hoped it would be a turning point in their relationship, but nothing ever came of it. I just don't understand your brother at all," she finishes with a disgusted shake of her head.

We talk for a few more minutes before I go upstairs to unpack. My suitcases are still sitting where I left them in my bedroom. I really need to get my own place now. I hear my phone chime in my purse, and I pull it out to find a text from Aidan.

Luc wants me to meet him and Max for a drink tonight. Pick you up afterward?

It's ridiculous how mushy a flipping text can make me feel. I'm supposed to be putting distance between us, not gushing like a teenager would over a text from her first boyfriend. *But that's what this feels like. New. Exciting.* I should say that I'm staying home tonight and make some excuse not to see him. Instead, my fingers fly across the screen.

Text me when you leave the bar. I'll drive to your place. Will need my car for work tomorrow.

I just manage to stop myself from adding a smiley emoticon. I'm so screwed. Would it be so bad, though? Does he really need to know my entire medical record to go out with me? Isn't the STD talk the extent of what you share with someone? It's not as if we're getting married tomorrow or anything that serious. We're simply spending time together, both in and out of bed. Perhaps I've been making this more complicated than it needs to be. After all, we may decide we can't stand each other, and that will be that. No need to start blurting out stuff that doesn't concern him. For the first time since my cancer diagnosis, I'm going to live in the moment and not worry about tomorrow. Don't I deserve some measure of normalcy? I feel a wave of relief at my decision, along with a nagging sense of something akin to guilt that I'm somehow deceiving the man I've come to care about, but I push it aside. It's just casual, right?

Aidan

"Tell me why we keep coming here?" I wince as I see Misty waving from behind the bar. "I barely made it out of here with my clothes on the last time."

Max Decker, Lucian's attorney and our friend, laughs.
"No kidding. She scares the hell out of me. I told her I was
engaged, and she offered to have a threesome. Said to bring
Rose in, she'd love to get to know her better." Raising a
brow, he adds, "I don't think she has any idea who she's
dealing with there. I doubt Rose has left home without
carrying a gun since she was five years old."

Lucian shrugs his shoulders as he returns Misty's wave.
"Yeah, she offered the same thing to me. Lia's actually met
her once, and she thought it was hysterical. She said
something like, 'good luck with that,' and chowed down on
her cheeseburger."

"She's been working with Rose every day for months
now, so that's bound to wear off on her soon," Max points
out.

"It's damn sure enough to make you keep your dick in
your pants, isn't it?" I smirk. I've no doubt Rose could
kick all of our asses if she wanted to.

Misty arrives at our table carrying a tray of beer and our
usual burgers. Her tiny shirt is struggling to contain her
huge tits, and I swear when she moves I think I see a
nipple. And those shorts. How in the hell does she even sit
down in them? They're so tight she must have to lie on the
bed to zip them up. She's rocking the big hair tonight and
could easily pass for an '80s rock slut. I've barely
processed these thoughts when our tray is on the table and
she's sitting on my lap. "Aidan. Holy shit, you're back.
Sugar, I've just missed you so much!" Before I can protest,
her mouth is on mine. My hands are flailing as I attempt to
move away from her. For such a tiny thing, she's
surprisingly strong. Her arms around my neck are like
fucking zip ties.

"Mis—ty, stop," I choke out as I desperately try to avoid
her tongue. Good Lord, the woman is mouth raping me
right here, and my two idiot friends are doing nothing but
laughing their asses off. I get to my feet thinking I'll shake
her off my lap, but I can't believe that she manages to hold

on. "Let—go," I wheeze out and finally see Luc stagger to his feet to help me out. He's laughing so fucking hard it takes him precious moments to regroup, but finally, he's prying her hands from around me.

"Misty, hon, let's give Aidan a chance to breathe. I'm sure he really appreciates your . . . warm welcome, but he's going through a shy phase. You might be overwhelming him a bit."

"Yeah, he's found Jesus lately and is doing the whole chastity vow," Max adds. "In another few months, he'll be a born-again virgin so don't derail that process."

That seems to get Misty's attention. She moves away from me as if she's just been told I have a scorching case of crabs. I swear she stares at my crotch for all of two minutes before shaking her head. "That explains so much, sugar." In a whisper that is more like a shout, she says, "I thought maybe something was wrong with your equipment. I've hugged you several times, and you've never been . . . excited." She stands up straight and thrusts her huge tits in the air. "And believe you me that never happens. Why didn't you just tell me that you were a virgin?" Fuck, every nearby table is riveted by this conversation. I might as well toss my man card on the floor and set the bastard on fire.

"I'm not," I hiss, but she cuts me off before I can finish defending myself.

She pats my arm as if I'm some damn poodle. "I think it's sweet, really I do. But I like my men with a little more experience. I'm not up to training someone green behind the ears. Now if you get yourself a woman and get that cherry popped, let me know. Then maybe I can work with that."

Luc shakes his head as if to tell me to take what she's giving me and keep my mouth shut. What choice do I have? If I say Max is lying, she'll be all over me again. In this bar, the lesser of evils is for Misty to believe that my cock has never seen the light of day before, much less a pussy. So I lower my head and do my best to look embarrassed. Actually, it's not that hard considering the amount of people who now think I've never fucked a woman. "Thanks for understanding," I mumble. My two dickhead friends look as if they'll fall on the floor in a fit of laughter at any moment, but Misty thankfully appears blissfully unaware.

She unloads her tray finally then gives one last shake of her head. I hear her say, "What a waste," under her breath as she walks away.

When she's out of earshot, I cross my arms and glare at Max. "A virgin, really? Where in the hell did that come from?"

He puts a hand over his mouth, smothering a grin. "Hey man, I panicked, and it's all I could come up with. It didn't exactly look like you were in the position to be picky with her sucking your tonsils out of your throat."

"I thought it was pretty good," Luc chokes out. "Did you see how fast she got away from you? I would have thought to someone like Misty that would have been as good as a green light. I'm amazed that she was that . . . repulsed."

"So this is what being a loser feels like," I say as I look around the bar. "I bet I couldn't pick up a single woman in this bar tonight even if I begged."

"Oh, I don't know." Luc inclines his beer bottle toward a table in the back. "Those cougars look mighty interested in bringing you into manhood. If I were you, I wouldn't walk that way. If you've got to take a piss, do it out front."

"Shit." I laugh, finally seeing the humor in what has just occurred. "I told you we need to stop coming to this place. Next time we have a guys' night, we're sticking to somewhere like Hooters. Those girls are professionals. They give you a pretty smile, shake their ass, and wait for the big tip. I've never been mauled by anyone from there."

Max takes a bite of his burger and then wipes his mouth before saying, "You should have just told us you were saving yourself for Kara Jacks. I thought we were all friends, but neither Luc nor I knew that you were . . . involved with her."

My good mood falters as I think of Kara's arms around me at my mother's funeral. I'd spent the day with my father, but as if by mutual agreement, we hadn't discussed my mom. Neither of us was ready for that. Instead, we'd worked in the yard, and then had lunch together at a local steakhouse. I had made sure the hospice care removed all the medical equipment and had a cleaning company clean the house from end to end while we were at the funeral. My father didn't need to be faced with that. As if sensing where my thoughts have gone, Luc claps a hand on my shoulder and squeezes. I actually want to hug him when he cracks a joke to lighten the mood. "You know if Kara hadn't dyed her hair, I would find it pretty damn weird that you're seeing my wife's twin. Hell, it's still strange." He thumps his fist lightly against my arm before adding, "I remember you hitting on Lia before we got married."

Both Max and I chuckle at his wry expression. I hold my hands up to protest my innocence. "I'll admit it's a little strange, and even Kara commented on it when we met in Charleston. But you gotta admit, they don't really resemble each other much anymore."

Luc looks skeptical. "I'll give you the benefit of the doubt on this one because I don't want to dwell on the alternative. So how exactly did you two meet and surpass the acquaintances stage?"

I shake my head. *Women in no way have the market cornered on gossip.* Men are every bit as nosy. "She was staying in Lee's house in Charleston, and I was just down the beach. We met in a bar one night and kind of hit it off. We hung out for a few weeks until I left."

"Sounds neat and tidy," Max interjects.

I know he wants to say more but doesn't want to keep referencing my mother's funeral, and I certainly don't want that either, so I find myself volunteering additional information. "We had dinner together every night after that.

We either cooked or dined at one of the local places. I enjoyed spending time with her; she made me laugh."

"You really like—like her, don't you?" Luc asks in surprise.

God, is this grade school? "Yeah, I guess I do. I didn't know if I'd see her again when I left. She seemed to want things to end at that point, but then she was there yesterday . . . and I don't know. We've decided to see where things go."

Max's jaw drops as he says, "You're saying you're going to date her? Like a relationship and the whole bit?"

I pick up one of the stale pretzels from the bowl in the middle of the table and toss it at him. *Surely, Max hasn't thought I've been celibate all these years while pining for Cassie? Would he really have no clue what I was up to during the first twelve months I was away?* So *not a virgin.* "Man, that's just insulting that you're so amazed. You do know I'm not actually the virgin you told Misty I was, right? I've entertained quite a few women through the years."

"Hookers don't count," Luc jokes.

"Fuck you," I deadpan. "Escorts aren't hookers, at least in Asheville. Hell, you should know that. I believe you met your lovely wife through one of those very services, didn't you?"

Luc grits his teeth. "Touché," he grumbles.

I enjoy the direct hit I've scored for a moment, before admitting, "I promised my mother I wouldn't close myself off to finding someone. She was convinced that Cassie wasn't 'the one' and she wanted me to keep an open mind. So when Kara reappeared and the attraction was still there, I decided to give it a go. I've come to care about her, and I want her in my life."

"I think that's great," Max says sincerely. "I certainly wasn't looking for a relationship when Rose came along. Hell, I fought it, but it happened anyway, and I'm damned glad. She may scare the hell out of me some days, but it's never boring." He grins.

Luc raises his beer bottle and motions for me to do the same. "I'm happy for you, brother. From what I know of Kara, she's the real deal. Have you met her parents yet?"

Luc looks vastly amused when I say, "No, I haven't. I was going to walk her in when I dropped her at home, but she didn't want me to."

"That should be an interesting family dinner. Think you can get us an invitation?" Max asks. "I bet Rose would fit right in with the Jacks family."

"All the stuff they say about them isn't true, right?" I ask warily. I look over at Luc. "You've spent time with Lia's father. Is his reputation blown out of proportion or do you think he's as dangerous as he's rumored to be?"

Luc takes his time before he answers. "The only thing I know for certain is that he loves his daughter, his granddaughter, and he tolerates me. He and his brother had an interesting childhood and did what was necessary to survive. The same as any of us would do. Unless there is a threat to my family, I don't want to know any more than that. Peter's supposed to be the nice one, so I wouldn't worry about him killing you over the pot roast. At least not right away," he adds and laughs when I flip him off.

As much as I'm enjoying my evening with my friends, I find myself checking my watch. I've missed Kara, and I'm ready to see her. I stick it out a bit longer, though, not wanting to be called a pussy for leaving so soon. Plus, there's no way I'm walking by Misty alone. She might have rethought her virgin aversion by now. I pull my phone out and text Kara while Max and Luc are arguing over baseball.

Home in an hour, princess. Have a dress on with no bra or panties. You're getting fucked as soon as you walk in the door.

Her reply comes just moments later and has my dick throbbing.

I'm sucking your cock first. Deal with it.
Absolutely perfect.

I wonder for a moment if my mother had any idea that I'd already met the one who would be important to me before our talk. Considering I had been reeling from her revelation about Cassie never owning my heart, I hadn't thought to mention Kara. But I think I felt it then. I wish I had told her about Kara. I wish I'd told her about numerous things, and now that chance was gone. *And that stings.* Thinking about her words spoken about a week ago now, I suck in a quick breath. *When you love someone, there should still be times you're together in simple ways that you treasure. Laughing over a joke. Remembering a smile over something silly. Countless moments captured in time that you play in your head like a movie when you're alone.* That's what it is like with Kara. We might not end up married with kids, but that doesn't mean we can't have a good relationship, one where we both benefit physically and emotionally. I'd like to think our relationship would give my mom a measure of peace. For now, she gives me exactly what I need: a new beginning. A new chapter.

Where the story goes, only time will tell.

Kara

I squeal as the door to Aidan's home swings open, and I'm jerked inside. He pushes me against the wall and runs a hand under the short dress I'm wearing. When he finds the bare skin of my ass, he groans his approval. "Good girl. You take direction well. Now, where shall I fuck you?" he asks almost idly. In another minute, he has me bent over a barstool, holding on to the cool metal. He flips the hem of my dress up and runs a palm across my cheeks before delivering a stinging slap. I draw in a harsh breath but don't object. He repeats this process another five times according to the running count in my head. Then he nudges his fingers between my legs and groans as he finds the wetness there. "You are so fucking perfect," he says as he strokes my slippery clit from behind.

"I believe I was supposed to suck your dick first," I choke out as I rock against his hand.

"You'll get my cock when I say you can have it," he says. "Right now, I want to bury it inside your wet pussy. Is that a problem for you, princess?"

He pushes what feels like two fingers deep, and I whimper. "No . . . God, no!" I cry out. "Now—"

I barely have time to finish my demand because he's there. His dick feels huge in this position, and I grit my teeth as my body protests his invasion. There's a twinge of pain, but on its heels is blinding pleasure. I've never been this full before. I don't know where he ends and I begin. I'm a mass of nerve endings alight with sensory overload. I attempt to thrust backward and create more friction, but he holds my hips, tightly controlling my movements. "You'll take what I give you, when I want you to have it," he growls as he drives me mad with shallow thrusts.

"Damn you!" I shriek. "Stop teasing and fuck me, Spencer!" I earn another smack on the ass for my tantrum, which just pushes me closer to the edge. A man has never spanked me before, and I love it when Aidan does. He's not hitting me hard enough to really hurt. It's the erotic nature of the act more than anything that turns me on. I want him to dominate me in this way. I crave it.

He pulls my ass cheeks farther apart, which allows him to go deeper when he thrusts hard. When his finger rims my ass, I'm done for. He barely has the tip inside before I'm coming and coming. "Goddamn, Kara," he shouts as he bottoms out in a series of deep plunges before I feel him release inside me. I lie there on the stool panting with his weight against my back and his cock still buried inside me. Even after coming, he's still hard. The man truly is a robot.

He could probably go again, but I'm done for. I want to do something insanely mushy right now like curl up and watch a movie together.

"One of us needs to move," I wheeze as his weight begins to limit my air supply.

He shifts away immediately, rubbing my back in apology. His dick slides out of me, and I feel wetness trickling down my legs. "Sorry, baby."

The sound of a phone ringing has me struggling to pull my dress down which is absurd since the caller can't see me. The sound doesn't appear to be coming from my nearby purse, though. "I think that's yours," I point out as he makes no move to locate his phone.

He scowls as it stops ringing, and then begins again almost immediately. He fumbles through his pants pockets until he comes up with it. I pity the person on the other line as he answers it with a curt, "Spencer." Then he stills and his eyes fly to mine. "Yes . . . this is Aidan. Um—no, sir, I'm not busy. What can I do for you?" He nods, still looking at me. "Yes, of course. That sounds great. Seven should work. I'll let her know. See you then."

He ends the call still staring at me; only now, he's scratching his head as if lost in thought. Exasperated, I ask, "Who was that, the president?" Why is he acting so strange?

"Worse." He grimaces. "It was your father inviting us for dinner tomorrow night. I don't suppose you know anything about that?"

My jaw drops and my lips move, but nothing comes out. And then I snort thinking how funny it is that the first time Aidan talks to my dad, his pants are around his ankles, and his magnificent cock is hanging out ready for more. *Of me.* And then I almost cry. I can't believe my parents are doing this. "I—no. I can assure you that I had no idea." I run a hand through my hair, trying to push the disheveled mess out of my face. "I'll call them back later and make some excuse. I know you don't want to meet them this soon."

Realizing how that sounds, I quickly add, "Or ever. I mean there may be no reason to meet them since we're just hanging out and that's a lot of pressure. Who says you have to ever see them at all, right? That's such an outdated thing. I bet people get married every day yet don't formally meet their girlfriend's family." *Oh God, why can't I stop?* "Not that I'm your girlfriend or expect that we'll ever get married. I was simply using that as an example. I don't want you to feel all pressured that I'm going to buy a scrapbook and start collecting wedding dress pictures and such." I laugh and even to my own ears, it sounds insane. *Kara, stop!* I say to myself, but I can't. "I'm not one of those women that try to Photoshop pictures of us together to see what our kids would look like. Oh! And subscribe to all of those destination wedding sites. Good Lord, I bet there are a million of those. I can't imagine anywhere being better than Charleston anyway. Plus, it would be the sentimental choice since we kind of got together there." Yet another crazy laugh flies from my lips as I quickly add, "But that's just on the tiny chance that we end up together, which I'm sure we won't. That—"

He's now leaning against the bar, sipping a beer, and I wonder where it came from. Did he actually go to the refrigerator and come back while I was rattling on and I didn't even notice? The smirk on his face says that he did. "You about done, princess?" he asks as his mouth twitches. "If you're gonna be a while, I'll grab some chips and salsa on the next trip. It would be nice, though, if you'd pause some so I don't miss anything while I'm gone."

"You're such a bastard," I grumble. "Why didn't you stop me? You must know by now that I'm incapable of doing it myself."

He raises his brows and grins. "You've gotta be kidding me. That shit right there is solid gold. It's as if you go into a trance or something. I'm just waiting for the day you get in the zone about my dick. Now that's something I'd like to hear you go on and on about for an hour. I bet it will be epic. Make sure you throw in a lot of references to it sliding into your pussy while you're at it. Then when I can't take it anymore, I'm going to stick my dick in your mouth and blow my load down your throat. Think that'll shut you up, baby?"

I walk past him and yawn dramatically. "Uh, maybe." I take off running down the hall toward the bedroom when he lunges at me. A few minutes later, he lives up to his threat, and his hard cock is indeed sliding between my lips. If he thinks it's some kind of punishment, though, he's sadly mistaken. I enjoy every minute of it.

CHAPTER ELEVEN

Aidan

I spent the day at the office starting the process of catching up on everything I missed in the past fourteen months. Lucian and Max had managed to close several deals I had in the works, and there were others in process I will be taking over. It's more comforting than I could have imagined to fall back into the familiar routine. I've always loved my job and hadn't realized how much I'd missed it. Plus being surrounded by those I think of as family helps me to cope another day without my mother. Even with Kara beside me, it's especially hard to wake up in the mornings, thinking all is right with the world for those few precious moments before it slams into me with the force of a brick wall.

She's really gone, and she's never coming back.

It's so fucking hard to believe. I still feel so much damned guilt over the time I wasted when I could have been spending time with her. At times, I rage against the cancer as if it's a real person that I could hurt with my words and thoughts. The only thing I get out of it, though, is bitterness, and I know if I continue, it'll overwhelm me.

Kara—sweet, beautiful, and slightly crazy Kara—has been a balm to my wounded spirit. She takes me away from the world and makes me forget everything except her. She sets my body on fire and fills me with laughter. She's a big reason I'm coping as well as I am. I'm not even freaked out about the family dinner in a few hours. Actually, she's more worked up about that than I am. I glance down at my watch and start packing away the papers from my desk. I have enough time to run by my dad's before I'm due at her house.

Luc left earlier to accompany Lia and Lara to the doctor for the little one's vaccinations. The poor bastard. I bet he's an absolute wreck by now. Lia should have probably taken Sam or Cindy instead. Lia had brought Lara by when they met Luc earlier, and I'd played blocks with her on the floor. I couldn't believe how much she'd grown. Of course, a year in kid time was almost a lifetime. It didn't take more than a few minutes, though, until I was eating out of the palm of her little hand again. Hell, if she'd been able to ask, I would have signed over the deed to my house and car on the spot. I even had a few crazy thoughts about Kara pregnant with my child. That should have been enough to break me out in a cold sweat, but oddly enough, I kinda liked it. We haven't used birth control the last few times we've had sex, but she told me in Charleston she was on the pill and had a recent STD check. I'd never trusted a woman's word for that in the past, but I knew Kara wouldn't lie about something like that.

I pull up at my dad's about fifteen minutes later and park behind his old Jeep Cherokee. I'd offered to buy him a new one a few years ago, but he wouldn't hear of it. He kept it in top running condition and said he didn't need some "fancy new car." I'm not going to lie; it's hard for me to walk in my childhood home now. Actually, it's almost suffocating, but I do it for him. How must he feel to live here after losing his wife? If he can handle it, surely I can for his sake. "Dad, it's me," I call out as I look around. The pictures of my mom gut me, and a part of me wants to pack them away where they won't hurt me as much. But that's not my decision, and would I be able to do it even if I did have the choice? Hell, it's hard to see her, but may be harder not to.

He walks out from the kitchen, wiping his hands on a dishtowel. "Hey, son. How was your first day back at work?" I study him closely and am relieved to see he appears okay. I'm not sure what I was expecting, but so far, everything is normal. I'd been worried that he would be upset that I hadn't returned to the house after the funeral. I hope in some small way he understands why I couldn't.

Nodding, I say, "Not bad. I've got a lot of catching up to do, but I'll get there. How about you? How was yours?" Even though his company had told him to take all the time he needed, he'd returned to work today as well. I didn't argue because I knew he needed the distraction like I did.

"Just the usual." He shrugs. "Faye dropped by when I got home. She was at the funeral, but we didn't get a chance to talk. She's offered to help me out with anything that needs to be done. She's one smart lady."

Surprised, I ask, "Lucian's Aunt Faye?"

Frowning, my dad says, "Well, of course. You know we've all been friends since you and Lucian met in school."

Faye Quinn had been like a mother to me when we were growing up. I spent almost as much time at her house as I did my own. She'd hugged me at the funeral, but that's about all I remember. The day was still a blur to me. *I don't think I will ever want to think about the day I buried my mother. Does anyone?* After my initial shock, I feel grateful she's stepped up to be there for my dad. I worry about him being alone so much, and hopefully, Faye will come around more now. "That's good," I say truthfully. "She's one of the good ones."

"Have you eaten yet?" he asks. "I was just about to heat something up for dinner."

My face goes hot. "Er . . . actually, I'm having dinner with Kara and her parents." I have no idea why that's embarrassing. Possibly because it's not the type of thing I've discussed with my dad since I was in high school.

He nods before taking a seat in his recliner. "That the girl you were with at the funeral?"

Shit, apparently all eyes were on Kara and me that day. Had anyone missed that? I perch on a nearby chair, clasping my hands loosely between my legs. "Yeah, her name is Kara Jacks. She's actually Lia's cousin. We met at Lia's graduation and again in Charleston."

His looks surprised when he asks, "And you're already at the meeting the parents stage?"

I shake my head. "I don't know what we're at. Her father called and invited me last night. I didn't really think no was an option even though it freaked Kara out. It's just dinner, though, right? I'm sure they're nice people who simply want to know who their daughter is spending time with."

A smile curves his lips. "I assume this girl isn't some teenager so the fact they're still that involved in her life says good things about them. You could use a woman like that. You need to branch out from these hourly girls."

"Wh—what? Dad! I don't do hookers. For God's sake." Shit, when did his opinion of me get so low?

He wrinkles his nose. "Hookers? What in Sam Hill are you talking about?"

"You said hourly," I point out, now just as confused as he looks.

"I meant women you only want to spend a few hours with because you've got nothing in common. Where in the world did you come up with hookers?" Lifting a brow, he asks, "You don't mess with those, do you? Asheville's a big city now, and I'm sure there are plenty of those types of women around. Nothing good comes from that, son," he adds sternly.

I pinch the bridge of my nose, fighting the urge to laugh. "I'll try to remember that, Dad." I smirk. The clock on the wall indicates I have about twenty minutes until I'm due at

Kara's, so I get to my feet. "I need to hit the road before I'm late. Want to go out for dinner tomorrow night? You pick the place."

"Sounds good to me. Why don't you bring your new girl along? I reckon it's time that I formally meet her as well."

"I'll ask her," I assure him. Shit. *Shit.* Does Dad feel hurt that I didn't introduce Kara to Mom before she died? He doesn't look hurt, but who can really tell when he's probably just functioning at the moment. Should I have introduced Kara to Mom? *Should I have told her about Kara? She wanted me to find true love, someone who would complete me. Shit.* But I didn't know if Kara would even allow me back into her life last week, and my heart had been breaking just thinking about Mom dying. I take a deep breath and try to stop my brain from spinning. "I'll call you tomorrow, and we'll finalize our plans. Let me know if you need anything before then, okay?" As I'm getting in my car, I grieve the apparent difference in my relationship with my father. How could it only be a few days since my mom has gone, yet I almost feel as though I'm the parent? But I also feel a closeness and kinship I haven't felt in years. We've survived the death of the most important person in our lives. We aren't strong enough yet to openly talk *about* her, but she's there just the same. My life seems to be changing faster than I can adapt. At the end of the day, though, I have no choice but to keep moving and hope that I've had my share of tragedy for a while.

Kara

"I still can't believe you called Aidan without telling me," I grumble to my father. I worked at Falco today attempting to fill in for Liza, and I'm exhausted. I'm also more than a little stressed over this unexpected dinner.

He shrugs as if to say he doesn't understand what the big deal is. "I was planning to fire up the barbecue tonight anyway. Your mother has a hankering for a hot dog, and I wouldn't mind a good burger. I figured we might as well kill two birds with one stone."

"Can we refrain from using the word 'kill' where Aidan's concerned?" I sigh. "He probably already thinks you and Uncle Lee are gangsters."

Looking vastly amused, he says, "You know that's absurd, honey. We retired from that years ago. I don't even think your uncle actually kills people anymore."

"Ha-ha." My mom elbows him in the side as she hands him the plate of burgers and hot dogs to grill. "All we need is that busybody Mrs. Collins next door hearing you joke about that. She already crosses herself when she sees you outside."

Clearing my throat, I put a hand out to stop my father before he moves away. "Please don't mention anything around Aidan about my . . . cancer."

He sets the plate he's holding down and leans against the counter. "You haven't told him?"

"It's nothing to be ashamed of, Kara," my mother adds. "Why wouldn't you want him to know?"

"He lost his mother to cancer just days ago. I didn't really think it was the best time to blurt out, 'Oh, what a coincidence. I've had cancer myself. It might even come back sometime. Fun, right?'"

"Kara," my father snaps, "don't even joke about that. I swear sometimes it's as if you hope that happens."

"Pete," my mother gasps out. "That's absurd. She's just trying to inject some humor into the situation."

"I'm sorry," I say quietly. "I shouldn't have said that. But you also need to understand that if I don't have some kind of sense of humor about what happened to me, then I'll crack from the pressure of worrying all the time."

My father opens his arms and motions for me to come to him. He enfolds me in a hug. "I'm sorry, kiddo. I guess it's still too fresh for your old man to deal with sometimes. And of course, we won't say anything to Aidan. That's your business to tell him when you want to. But if you like him, then don't wait too long. He should know what a brave woman you are and what you've endured."

We pull apart when the doorbell sounds. My father makes as if he's going to run to answer it. We end up racing through the house, and I'm winded as I throw the door open to a startled Aidan. "Well, hello," I purr, which actually comes out as more of a pant.

He steps forward and drops a kiss on my mouth. "Hey, princess. What were you up to before you answered the door?"

My father steps up behind me. "She was trying to keep me from getting here first. I have no idea why." Aidan pulls me to his side so he can take my father's extended hand. "It's good to see you again, Aidan. I'm glad you could make it."

"I appreciate the invitation, sir," Aidan replies smoothly.

My father waves away the formal greeting. "Call me Pete. Come on in. I was just firing up the grill. How about we let the ladies handle the kitchen, and you and I man the backyard?" I give Aidan a grimace, but he just rubs my arm reassuringly as we follow my father through the house. "You remember my wife, Charlotte, don't you? I think we all met briefly at Lia's graduation."

Aidan steps forward and drops a kiss onto my mother's cheek. "It's a pleasure to see you again. May I call you Charlotte?"

My mother is blushing like a schoolgirl as she fawns over him. "Well, of course, Aidan. Welcome to our home. It's wonderful to see you again. Kara's had so many nice things to say about you."

I have? Boy, is she laying it on thick. We've barely discussed Aidan, but by the way she's going on about it, he probably thinks I've been stalking him for years. Good grief. Luckily, my father drags him outside to say God knows what to him. This may be the last night I see him because he's likely to run if he survives the evening. "What was all of that?" I ask my mother when the door closes behind them.

She gives me that innocent expression that none of us ever believe. "What? I was just trying to make him feel comfortable." Lowering her voice, she whispers, "And if I can help you close the deal, then why not? Did you see how he was looking at you?"

Putting my hands on my hips, I hiss, "Yeah, like he wanted to be anywhere but here." I give her a thumbs up. "If you wanted to get rid of him, then good job."

My father opens the door, ending our conversation. "Hey, how about bringing some beer out when you come?"

"I'll get them, Daddy," I offer, taking the opportunity to rescue Aidan. I'm not sure what I expected, but when I walk out to the back patio, he and my father are laughing it up like best friends.

I hand my father a beer and then give one to Aidan. "Thanks, babe," he says easily as he throws an arm over my shoulders and pulls me to his side. *Okay, PDA is obviously not a problem for him.* Instead of stabbing Aidan with a sharp object for touching his daughter, my father just beams his approval. I swear I'd almost think he was high or something. Since when has he let anyone off this easily?

I'm actually nice and relaxed by the time we sit down to eat. Therefore, I almost choke on my hamburger when my mother asks, "Have you ever been married, Aidan?"

His beer bottle freezes halfway to his mouth as he looks at her warily. Apparently, I'm not the only one who'd let down their guard a bit too much. "Er . . . no, I haven't."

She nods thoughtfully before adding, "Have you ever been close? Maybe lived with someone or had a child with them?"

Holy shit, what is she doing? "Mom, I don't think—"

Aidan puts a hand on my leg under the table, halting my protests. "No, I don't have children, nor have I ever lived with a woman. I lost someone last year from my past who I cared about a great deal, but we were never romantically involved."

My mother reaches across the table and puts her hand over his. "I'm so sorry to hear that. I didn't mean to bring up painful memories."

"It's fine, Charlotte," he says graciously. I resist the urge to kick my mother's foot under the table. Aidan takes us all by surprise when he adds, "Kara's actually the first woman I've been involved with in a long time. I'm looking forward to seeing where our relationship goes."

What the hell? Can he see me melting into a puddle at his feet? My mother looks as if she's just been handed her Christmas present early, and even my father appears unusually pleased. Then I realize they've all turned to look at me as if awaiting my reaction. *Shit, what do I say?* Finally, I settle for a, "Me too." I throw in a bright smile when they don't look away, and that seems to do it. Aidan squeezes my knee, and I put my hand on top of his.

"We were so very sorry to hear about your mother passing away," my mother says. I know she feels as if she must make some mention of it, but couldn't she have waited until later?

Aidan clears his throat, and I know he's struggling. "Thank you. It's been a tough time for my father and me, but we're making it."

"Oh, honey." My mother is all but gushing now. "You've got a family right here whenever you need us. Right, Pete?"

My father nods as he chews his burger. When he's swallowed his bite, he says, "Absolutely. Welcome to the family, son."

And there we are, folks. The stalker and her insane family. I've known Aidan all of one minute, and we've spent most of that time fucking each other's brains out. My family is rolling out the welcome mat very prematurely. He must think we're crazy. Maybe this is some kind of reverse psychology on their part. Instead of trying to intimidate him, they're going the opposite way in an attempt to get rid of him. Thankfully, the rest of the meal is uneventful, and I manage to drag Aidan out of the house before my mother starts discussing sex and his net worth. "I'm so sorry about that." I cringe as we're standing next to his car.

He chuckles as he pulls me close. "It was fine, princess. I enjoyed myself." I give him a skeptical look, but he doesn't take his statement back. "Want to ride with me to the apartment? I can drop you off in the morning on my way to the office."

I want to say yes so badly, but I feel as if I need this one night of space to work through what's happening between us. We've been attached at the hip for the last few days, and truthfully, I'm not used to that type of closeness with a man. "I need to stay home tonight. I haven't unpacked my things from the beach, and I'm pretty much out of clothes." He looks so disappointed that I almost take it back, but instead of arguing, he kisses me gently on the lips, and then on the forehead.

"All right, princess. Do what you need to do. I'll call you tomorrow, okay?"

I nod and attempt to swallow the lump in my throat as he gets in his car and pulls away. I wave then walk back toward the house. I'm on my own for the evening just as I planned. But why do I not feel as though I have won here? The *victory* is hollow. Just like when I evaded our connection when he left Charleston, Aidan didn't fight me on my need for space. It's as if he understands me, and knows I need time to process my thoughts and actions. *How can that be possible? He was supposed to be a fling. A sexy, multiple-week fling that stayed in Charleston.*

He loved Cassie for nearly twenty years. Probably still does. *He's not fickle.*

He stuck by Lucian throughout the awful times of his life. He's incredibly kind. And incredibly strong. *He's loyal.*

I could practically feel his pain tonight when Mom mentioned his mom's death. *He loves so deeply.*

Yet he'd patiently accepted my parents' condolences. Seemed genuinely thankful for my dad's offer of extended family. *He's respectful.*

He's passionate both in and out of the bedroom. Despite his dominant hand and assertive lovemaking, *he's selfless.*

I realize in a moment of blinding clarity that I've fallen in love with Aidan Spencer. No matter how many times I tell myself it's too soon, there's no escaping the fact.

What in the hell am I going to do about it?

CHAPTER TWELVE

Aidan

A client held me up this afternoon, and now, I'm running late to meet Kara. Tonight is our two-month anniversary, and we're having dinner at Leo's to celebrate. Fuck, I never thought I'd see the day when I'd be celebrating an anniversary, period, much less one measured in months. But what wouldn't I do for the woman who has taken everything in my life and made it better? She's a dirty-talking, sassy-mouthed handful who keeps me on my toes. Hell, I never know what's going to come out of that mouth next, and it turns me on like you wouldn't believe.

I spend an absurd amount of time fucking her, and when I'm not inside her, I'm thinking of ways to get there again in the least amount of time. It's not only the sex that keeps me hooked, though. I've never enjoyed just spending time with a woman the way I do her. I love to do lame shit like read the Sunday paper together in Starbucks while she sips one of those frou-frou drinks she likes. I paint her fucking toenails. If that doesn't say whipped, I don't know what does. We're even talking about getting a dog together. That's about as close to a commitment with a woman as I've ever been.

Just thinking about my time with her makes me remember my mother telling me that I was never truly happy around Cassie, and when I found a woman I truly loved, the difference would be obvious. *My mom.* How I miss her. Her wisdom. Her love. Her strength and kindness. I can't believe it's been two months since she died. When my dad met Kara at dinner that first time, I thought I saw tears in his eyes at moments. And then when Kara went to the bathroom, he grabbed my hand and said, "Aidan, your mother would have loved Kara so much." We both had tears in our eyes then, and as he spends more time with her, I can see the wistfulness in his expression. He misses his soul mate. I thought Cassie was my soul mate, but I can appreciate my mom's words so much more now. I didn't really believe it at the time, but now, the moments I spend with Kara are so vastly different and better than my happiest moments with Cassie. Sometimes, it makes me bitter that I spent so much time loving an imaginary version of Cassie. I see now that I wanted her to be someone she wasn't. I grew up thinking that if she'd only give me a chance I could make her happy. I realize now that nothing could have helped her. She wasn't capable of being happy. I'll have to forever live with the guilt of not being able to save her, but I don't have to throw the rest of my life away wishing for something that was never meant to be.

Kara has helped me see there can be more to life than I ever realized. A one-night stand never felt as good as coming home to a woman I care about. I take the good-natured ribbing from my friends with a smile because I'm fucking happy for the first time in my adult life. I used to marvel at how different Lucian was after meeting Lia. Now, I completely understand it. The right woman is a game changer. I'm not even freaked out about the fact that I'm in love with her. I haven't said the words to her yet, but I feel them. I just don't want to come on too strong, too soon. She's still a bit skittish because she's never been involved in a serious relationship either. At times, I think there might be something more to it than that, but she hasn't been forthcoming, so perhaps I'm imagining things. I can't really blame her. I've no desire to be one of those couples who feel they have to know every bit of the other's past. It does nothing but breed insecurities and doubts. There's no way in hell that I want to make a list of every woman I've had sex with. Shit, I couldn't if I tried. And I certainly don't want to know every man who's fucked my girl. That would drive me insane. Therefore, I accept she may not be ready to share some things. I trust in her character. I don't feel wary around her like I did Cassie. Cassie was . . . darkness. Kara is light.

I pull up to the valet stand and see her leaning against the building in a form-fitting black pencil skirt and a white silk blouse. She's wearing a chain belt that emphasizes her tiny waist and curvy hips. Fuck, I love her body. She's mentioned changing her hair back to her natural blond, but I don't know if either Luc or I are ready for that yet. I still think it would be too weird to sleep with a woman who looked so much like Lia. She glances down at her watch when I approach and then rolls her eyes. I lean in and kiss her neck, whispering, "I'll spank that ass when we get home for that."

She puts her arm around my waist and murmurs, "I'm counting on it."

My cock is rock hard, and she giggles as I arrange my slacks. "You're pure evil, princess." I sigh. I open the door to the restaurant, put my hand on the small of her back, and lead her inside. I've reserved a private table in the corner, one that Luc normally requests as well. I shudder to think of what's gone on under the cover of the tablecloth between those two. She slides into the booth next to me, and I smile as I realize I'm like all those other people I used to mock for leaving half the table empty and sitting side by side instead.

We order the lasagna for two and then settle back in our chairs with a glass of wine. She touches my arm. "How was your day, babe?"

She has no idea how much I love that she always cares enough to ask about the little stuff like that. My dinner interactions with women have mostly consisted of verbal foreplay before a round of hard fucking. I had never bothered to inquire about their lives because frankly, I hadn't cared. It was sex, pure and simple. "Hectic but good. How about you? How did Jen go taking on the Blackwell account today?"

She smiles. "Really well. She's picking up things so quickly. I swear Liza was a machine. Jen is great, but Liza made everything seem so easy. She must have worked herself into the ground every day. I had no idea she handled so much. And why is Uncle Lee being such a stubborn ass?" she grumbles. "It's been nearly three months since Liza resigned, and it's obvious to everyone he's lost without her. Yet he won't admit it."

"Are you sure those two haven't been mixing business with pleasure? This sounds more like a lover's tiff than an office disagreement."

"I don't know, but I've been thinking the same thing," she admits. "I mean it's pretty obvious that Liza liked him, and Lee was different with her than other employees. I have no idea if they've ever officially crossed that line, but if not, I bet they've both certainly thought about it."

Our bread and salads arrive, and I take a bite before saying, "Have you thought about trying to contact Liza again? Perhaps she's ready to talk to someone by now and would talk to another woman more easily."

"She hasn't returned my calls, Aidan. She'll talk when she wants to."

She sounds frustrated, and I put my arm around her shoulders and kiss her forehead. "She has to come home eventually. You should tell Lee that maybe Liza is waiting for him to show up. Talk is cheap when it's all you've ever received. It may be time for him to piss or get off the pot."

"That's lovely." She giggles. "I'm such a lucky woman."

I puff out my chest and wink. "Damn straight you are, princess. It's all first class with me, and you know it." We tease each other throughout our meal. Our plates are cleared away, and we're enjoying a piece of chocolate pie when I slide my hand into my pocket and pull out a jeweler's box. Her eyes go wide, and I see her nervously swallow. "Calm down, princess, I promise there's no ring in here. But it's such an ego boost to know how terrifying you find that prospect," I add wryly.

She gives me an apologetic smile before holding her hand out impatiently. "Well, give it here then. Or do you have some flowery words you'd like to deliver first?"

I shake my head at her teasing and put the box in her hand. Suddenly, I'm a bit embarrassed. "I wanted to get you something to mark our two months together. I know that's kind of a pussified thing to do, but I saw this in the window at Heller's when I was walking by the other day, and it seemed like something you'd like." Dear God, I made an absolute mess out of that. Since when have I been anything other than smooth? Certainly not just then as I'd stumbled through my carefully prepared speech. Yeah, I'd butchered the thing. I'm surprised she isn't laughing her ass off now instead of looking just a tad bit teary eyed. Maybe she's crying because it *was* that damn bad. "I swear if you start crying I'm returning it," I threaten and am relieved to see her turn to glare at me.

"Can you stop talking for five minutes, please? I'm trying to enjoy this moment, and you're ruining it for me," she huffs. She pops open the lid, and I hear her inhale deeply as she stares down at the platinum heart pendant encrusted with small diamonds. It winks brightly even in the dim light of the restaurant and looks almost as expensive against the velvet as it was. "Oh Aidan," she whispers as once again she appears near tears. "It's beautiful, babe, I love it."

I move her hands aside and gently remove the delicate chain from the box before motioning for her to turn so I can fasten it around her neck. Her fingers immediately reach to outline the heart as it settles against her skin. Then something happens that leaves me speechless. She throws her arms around me and says, "I love *you*, Aidan." I can barely make out the rest of her words against my neck. But what I do hear has me biting my lip to keep from laughing. "Know it's probably too soon. There's no set time that you wait because I googled it. Hope it doesn't freak you out. I should have let you say it first, right? It just came out, but we can pretend I didn't say it first. Not that I expect for you to say it now or anything. Don't feel as if I'm pressuring you. It's not because of the necklace either. Thank you. I do love it by the way. I'll never take it off. Well, only when it needs to be cleaned. Or If I break the clasp. I'll be careful, though. Did you get the insurance? I'm really hard on jewelry, and it looks expensive. Wow, you smell really good." She then stops talking for a blessed moment to sniff my neck.

I take advantage of the distraction to pull her away. I laugh because her eyes are closed, and her nose is twitching. Apparently, she loves the cologne I'm wearing. Either that or she's gone to sleep. "Princess," I say softly. Her eyes drift open slowly as if she's in a daze. I rub my thumb across her bottom lip to hopefully keep her silent. "I love you too, and I'm fine that you were the first to say it. I have for a while, but like you, I felt the time was right tonight to let you know."

Her lip trembles against my finger and tears track down her cheeks. "You do?" she mumbles as she pushes my hand away.

"Absolutely, beautiful." I kiss her nose then her lips. "Now, let's get out of here and I'll show you exactly how much."

We're waiting for the check when a woman walks up to the table grinning as if she knows us. She doesn't look at all familiar to me, but I see the exact moment Kara recognizes her. She looks almost panicked, and I instinctively lay a hand on her leg. I'm ready to bodily remove the stranger from the restaurant for upsetting her. "Kara. I thought that was you. My husband and I were having dinner, and I saw you when we stood to leave. It's been so long. How are you doing?"

"Er—hi, Jody. It's good to see you. I'm doing very well." Kara still looks extremely uncomfortable and almost nervous. Who is this woman?

I get to my feet and extend a hand. "I'm Aidan Spencer, Kara's boyfriend, and you are?"

The other woman slaps a hand against her head and giggles. "Oh, where are my manners? I'm Jody Townsend." We shake hands. She *seems* harmless enough, which is why I can't figure out the strange vibe coming from Kara. Maybe Jody is actually a raving bitch but keeping it under wraps around me. Whatever, I'm ready for her to move along and not ruin our evening.

"And how do you know Kara?" I ask politely. I really don't care, but she's still standing there, and Kara hasn't attempted to add anything.

"Jody," Kara blurts out in a voice laced with warning.

I turn to stare at her questioningly as Jody says, "Kara and I met while we were having radiation therapy. We bonded during our breast cancer treatment." I turn in shock to stare at the other woman, but she seems oblivious. "After the first week, we made all of our appointments at the same time so we had someone to talk to. I just hate we lost touch afterward." She looks around me to Kara as she adds, "I tried to call you a few times but never heard back. I was really worried, so I'm happy to see you looking so well. You're still in remission, right?"

Kara's eyes are locked on mine as she nods to Jody. My mind is reeling, and I can hardly make sense of what I'm

hearing. *Breast cancer? Remission? What the fuck?* I think
it's all a mistake at first, but the look on Kara's face says
it's not. She's terrified. "Aidan," she whispers, holding her
hand out toward me. Jody, thank God, appears to have
finally figured out that something is off and has made
herself scarce. But the damage is already done.

I'm on autopilot now as I take my wallet from my slacks
and peel off some bills to toss on the table. Then I turn and
make my way to the front door. I don't draw a breath until
I'm on the sidewalk. *What the fuck just happened?* The
door bursts open and Kara stands there. Her eyes are huge
on her pale face. I want to walk away so badly, but I can't
make myself leave her on the sidewalk. Regardless of how
she neglected to tell me about her cancer, I'd never recover
if something happened to her. *Can't. Do. That. Again.* I
hand the valet my ticket and wait. She looks as if she's
going to bolt at any moment. When the car is idling at the
curb, I open the passenger door and wave my hand for her
to get in. For a moment, I think she'll refuse, but she slowly
moves toward me and into the vehicle. I slam the door
harder than necessary and then get in the driver's side. "I'll
drop you at home," I say woodenly.

"Aidan—I was going to tell you, I just didn't know how.
I didn't want to get close to you because I knew you
wouldn't want me if you knew. Then you lost your mother
to cancer and I—what could I say to you? I fell in love with
you almost from the beginning. But you'd already lost so
much." She's crying now. The sound of her sobs fill the
car. *I'm barely breathing.*

I feel nothing. I can't—*won't*—allow myself to.
Stoically, I say, "You lied to me this whole time. You just
admitted that you knew how I'd feel yet you continued to
deceive me. Granted, I don't have much experience with
love, but that's not what I'd classify as loving."

"I couldn't help it if I had cancer, Aidan," she cries out.
"What—I'm not allowed to have someone in my life now
because I was sick at one time? Don't you think *I've*

suffered enough? Because if you don't think I have, I'll be more than happy to tell you about everything I've gone through."

"Really?" I snap. "Where was *this* honesty a few months ago? If you're so happy to tell me now, why not then?"

The air in the car vibrates with energy as we both toss out angry words. "I wasn't aware I owed you the details of my entire medical records to date you. I mean, should I confess to anyone I date that I had cancer at one time?"

"I'm not just *any man,* Kara. And I would think that you would tell me of all people. I'll give you a pass on not telling me in Charleston, but what about later on? You knew I lost my mother to the disease. Wouldn't anyone in that circumstance at the very least feel compelled to admit they'd battled the same thing? The fact you didn't . . . Did you set out to deceive me? You probably thought *this poor sap lost the love of his life a year ago and now his mother. Hey, I bet he's ripe for the picking. I won't bother to tell him that I've also had my own brush with death and not to get too attached.*"

"You fucking bastard," she screams. "Do you not hear the things you're saying to me? Have you any idea how hard it's been for me since the diagnosis? I had a breast cut off, Aidan. Do you know what that does to a woman? I had to go around for months with one side of my fucking bra empty! But lucky me—they fixed me right up with a new one. And I hate it. I know it doesn't belong on my body. Again, though, I'm so *fortunate* at how well things went for me. They chopped my tit off. I had my radiation, and then I was in remission. Plus, I get to sit around every single day for the rest of my life wondering when or if it's going to come back again. My parents enjoy it as well. We all love walking on eggshells waiting for one of them to crack the fuck open and bring the whole nightmare back once again. So yeah, in my spare time, I look for a guy to fall in love with and trick into thinking I'm a normal woman. Gotta get those kicks somehow, right?" she adds bitterly before falling silent.

We're pulling into the driveway of her parents' home now, and the silence between us is thick and oppressive. I put the car in park and struggle for the words I want to say. Finally, I slump back against my seat and let out a weary sigh. "I'm sorry. I could have worded all of that a lot better. But the whole thing caught me off guard, and I lashed out without thinking. I know you've suffered," I add quietly. "I was with my mother enough to see how hellish it can be." I don't think I could ever watch someone I love go through what my mom went through. *It was agony. Pure agony.* "You should have told me of all people, though."

"I never planned to let things go this far," she whispers. "When you left Charleston that was supposed to be it. That's why I didn't return your texts. I knew you wouldn't want me if you found out. I was developing feelings for you that couldn't possibly lead to anything but what it has now. But when Uncle Lee told me about your mom, and I heard she'd passed away, I wanted to be here for you. Just in case you wanted me. So I came to the funeral, and we connected even more than we had in Charleston. After that, I was terrified of losing *you.*"

My eyes are watering as I ponder the seeming hopelessness of our relationship. I look out the window trying to process this bombshell.

Kara had breast cancer. Fucking. Cancer.

I miss my mom. Moments like these, when I feel so confused, angry, and lost, I need her so much. Losing her has wrecked me, and I can't imagine ever going through that again. Watching my dad struggle to work out how to move forward has been agonizing. If I stayed with Kara, would that be me in a few years? It feels as if the entire thing has been built on lies, and God knows I can't go through that again. I love her, but . . . *I can't.* Fuck.

"Kara, another man might be able to handle this, but that's not me. I know it makes me the biggest jerk imaginable, but I simply don't have the strength left to lose another woman I love."

"But I'm fine now," she argues weakly. "I've been cancer-free for over a year."

I take her hand in mine and squeeze it. "And you can't imagine how happy I am to know that. But I can't sit around and wonder when or if it will come back. Maybe if I hadn't just lost my mom to the very same thing . . . I've never felt so helpless and powerless before and that's saying something after losing Cassie the way I did. I couldn't save her. There was no fighting *that* disease. It took control, and all I could do was watch as she faded a little more each day."

"I love you. Doesn't that count for anything?" she asks in a voice full of dejection.

My heart contracts painfully, and I die a little more inside as I turn her away. *I can't do this. I can't stay with her knowing her cancer might come back.* In sickness and in health. That's what my dad and mom swore to each other, and he was able to love her through sickness. I'm not that strong. Not yet. Maybe I'll never be. Maybe I'll never have the capacity to love like my dad loved my mom, or like Lucian loves Lia. I just don't think it will be . . . I just don't think I have that sort of love . . . *Fuck. This hurts.* "I love you too, but sometimes, that's not enough." I turn my head to look out the window again as I struggle for composure. I hear her moving around, and then something cold touches my hand. I look down to see the necklace I'd given her earlier. "No, Kara, I want you to have this," I protest as I attempt to give it back.

She opens her door before turning back to say, "I don't want it. The man who gave me that said he loved me. But I found out he only meant as long as I was in good health. At the first sign of anything else, he wanted out." Her words cut me like a knife, and I watch helplessly as she gets out of the car and shuts the door. *SHIT.* I punch the steering wheel wishing it would somehow heal the agony. After a few more minutes, I put the car in gear and drive away. What had begun as an evening filled with excitement and hope for the future is now nothing more than sorrow and disappointment. Once again, I've lost the woman I love. The only difference is that this time I willingly pushed her from my life. *Why the fuck do I keep losing?*

Kara

I'm absurdly grateful that my parents are nowhere to be seen as I stumble through the foyer and up the stairs to my room. I shut and lock the door before collapsing onto my bed in the dark. I fully unleash the sobs I've been attempting to hold back and let them soak the pillow I'm clutching. Never in a million years could I have imagined how tonight would turn out. So few people actually knew about my cancer that I hadn't thought someone like Jody would be the one to tell Aidan.

And it was every bit as bad if not worse than I could have imagined. At first, he'd been so angry, and strangely, that had been easier to handle. By the time we reached my house, he'd been as dejected as I was. He loves me; I don't doubt that. But as I had feared, he can't bring himself to deal with the risks of loving a cancer *survivor*. I know it could return, especially within the first five years. But what am I supposed to do, close myself off to the world? Don't I have a right to fall in love and be happy? Should I remain alone for years until statistics determine my chances of recurrence are lessened?

I want to be angry with him. It would be so much easier for me if I could turn my love into hate. But I did this to myself. Who else can I blame? Aidan went into this thinking he was getting a whole person. I never gave him any indication that I'm damaged goods. And he was right when he said that some men could handle my past, but not one who'd so recently lost not one, but two people he loved. His words were callous and hit their mark. But I invited them when I didn't tell him the truth. A month ago, we could have parted as friends. But now, I don't even have that.

I've lost him. Completely lost him.

What do you do when you've been hurt so badly you shouldn't be able to survive it? How does one go on when they give their heart to another only to lose that person? In a morbid way, it would almost be easier if he were dead. But I know that if something happened to him, it would break me apart completely. Then I wouldn't have to live each day knowing he's just across town living his life without me. *Sleeping with other women and putting me in his past. Giving his heart to someone whole.* The thoughts barely cross my mind before I'm desperately trying to take them back.

I hope that eventually I'll be strong enough to wish him a happy life. But for now, I curl up into the fetal position and curse the cancer that has now taken everything from me.

What's left to live for anymore?

CHAPTER THIRTEEN

Aidan

I'm having yet another pity dinner with Luc and Lia tonight. In the few months that Kara and I have been apart, these have become a weekly occurrence. I hadn't planned to tell anyone why we'd broken up, but one night, I'd wandered into the bar where Misty works, which should tell you something about my state of mind, and I'd gotten completely wasted. She'd managed to track Luc down, and he'd shown up. What had followed had been straight out of a country song. I was drunk and literally crying into my booze while I told him all about my busted love life. He hadn't tried to convince me that I was wrong. He'd simply listened and then took me to his place to sleep it off. I'd been woken the next morning by Lara standing in front of me poking me in the nose. The next week, the dinners had started. I never admitted it, but I was pathetically grateful for those hours with friends since that was pretty much the extent of my social interactions.

Lia opens the door and gives me a once-over before motioning me inside. I lean down and kiss her cheek, feeling my heart lurch at her resemblance to Kara. "Good to see you, sweetheart. You're looking beautiful as always." I used to joke with her about leaving Luc and running away with me, but I can no longer bring myself to do it. She looks so much like Kara that it feels wrong.

She smiles softly. "Thanks, Aidan. You, on the other hand, appear to have lost some weight. Aren't you eating?"

I do love this girl even if she doesn't pull any punches where I'm concerned. We're too much like brother and sister now to worry about social niceties. I shrug before giving her a sheepish grin. "I'm on more of a liquid diet now. Those calories seem to burn quickly at the gym."

She puts her hands on her hips and glares at me. "I assume we're not talking protein shakes here. Do you know how much I want to shake some sense into you right now? You're miserable, and Kara has pretty much just given up. Tell me how you're better off like this? You're scared of losing her, yet she's a few miles down the road. And she's not doing any better than you are. For God's sake—"

"I thought I heard you two," Luc interrupts as he walks up behind his wife. He gives me a look over her head that says I owe him for saving me from her wrath. "Lara is getting impatient for dinner."

"She's already eaten," Lia says absently.

Luc pulls Lia back against him. "Well then, she wants dessert."

The munchkin in question comes toddling up to us and promptly wraps her arms around one of my legs. I feel the drool sinking through the fabric of my slacks, but I couldn't care less. I lean down to pick her tiny body up and swing her into my arms. Her delighted squeals have us all laughing. "How's my most favorite girl in the whole wide world doing?"

She grins as she babbles, "Da da."

Luc snorts as Lia giggles. "Shhh, don't tell anyone, sweetie," I whisper loudly to Lara.

Lia rolls her eyes and promptly bursts my bubble. "She says the same thing to Sam and the mailman. I'm afraid you're just one of many baby daddies to her."

I stick out my tongue at Lia, which seems to fascinate Lara as she tries to grab it. I perform some evasive maneuvers as I tell Lia, "Thanks a lot. Way to make a guy feel special. Luc, you should keep a better eye on the little woman."

We finally make it to the dining room and my stomach grumbles as I see a heaping mound of spaghetti with meatballs awaiting us. "Just for you." Lia smirks knowing my love of pasta.

I sit Lara in her chair and grab Lia to twirl her around. "I take back everything I said. You're a goddess and if you want to have multiple sugar daddies, then you absolutely should."

The rest of the evening is lighthearted and fun as it always is with my favorite family. When it's time to leave, it's as though the muscles of my heart begin to atrophy. My empty apartment is all that I have waiting for me. Even though she was there for a short amount of time, Kara's presence seems to be all around me, and I find myself not wanting to go home. I haven't been able to throw away the dress-up tiara I bought her as a joke. *"For my very own princess, because every princess needs her own tiara."* My princess. Not anymore. That's one of the reasons I've spent far too many nights drinking. On the drive home, I wonder as always what she's doing tonight. Lia says she's miserable without me, but is she really? Maybe she's moved on and found someone who can love her in sickness and in health. I wish I were that man. I often wonder if I've sacrificed both our happiness for my own selfish need to protect my heart from further hurt. At this point, I no longer know.

Kara

I have a secret that may very well kill me, but I'm incapable of caring. Don't. Give. A. Shit. My depression is firmly in control and the antidepressants take away any panic I might have otherwise felt. I've lost count of the weeks since Aidan left me. Every day is a repeat of the last, even the weekends. I go to work and do my best to fill in for the still-absent Liza. Thankfully, Jen has most of the tasks under control. One of the benefits of having no outside life is that I've been able to dedicate myself to my job, and I've finally gotten the hang of it. Things are running smoothly at Falco once again, and I think that Uncle Lee has probably never been sadder. He misses Liza, and the absence of chaos seems to drive home she's not coming back. Yet like all men, he continues to cling stubbornly to his belief that he doesn't need her. I love him, yet I want to strangle him some days.

I even work weekends, which is no longer necessary. But it beats staying at my new apartment and enduring the worried glances my parents give each other when they think I'm not looking. If only they knew, they'd be freaking out and so very angry with me. But . . . it's my life, and I'll live it as I see fit.

Then there's the part of me that still checks the Internet for any mention of Aidan. Like a junkie hooked on her favorite form of crack, I can't get him out of my system, and I can't imagine a twelve-step program could accomplish it either. I shamelessly quiz Uncle Lee about Luc and Lia in hopes he'll mention Aidan, but it happens so rarely. Seeing Lia has been too hard. Watching her much-deserved happiness and knowing I'll probably never know that again. It's strange to me that I could care so very little about anything else in my life, including myself, but I can't let him go. He haunts my dreams and shadows my days. I ache to see him smile at me again in that way that made me feel special. I hunger for his body, remembering the way it owned mine. Sometimes, I think if I could just hear his laughter one more time, I'd be content to let go, but I know it would just make me thirst for more. I've ceased blaming him for leaving me. I am a ticking time bomb, and he would be crushed to know how right he was. *Or maybe he'd feel relieved. Glad he hadn't taken the risk.*

It's Friday and well after seven in the evening. Everyone has mostly left for the day, but as usual, I linger over tasks that are in no way pressing, but I need the busyness of work. When the phone rings, I remember that I forgot to switch it over to the after-hours voicemail. "Falco Industries, Lee Jacks's office, may I help you?" I ask on autopilot. I speak this same greeting at least a hundred times a day. My uncle is a busy man and receives a ton of calls, most of which will never get through to him.

"Kara Jacks please," says a masculine voice. I'm also used to this. Many who want to do business with Lee try to force a friendship with me, thinking it will help. Which it doesn't.

"This is Kara, how may I help you?" I'm grateful for the earpiece I'm wearing that allows me to continue working on the spreadsheet I'm finishing.

"Kara, this is Dr. Finley. I'm glad I was able to catch you. Are you free to speak for a moment?"

I freeze in my seat, and then my eyes dart around the empty reception area. It's on the tip of my tongue to make an excuse, but it's better to take this call in privacy rather than to risk my parents overhearing me. "Sure," I reply. "What can I do for you, Dr. Finley?"

He doesn't bother with more pleasantries. "Kara, I'd like to know why you haven't scheduled your biopsy yet. You of all people know that time is of the essence in these situations. I would think that, if nothing else, you would want to set your mind at ease. The lump may very well be benign. I see that almost as much as I see malignant ones."

Dammit. His words threaten to pierce my indifference, and I struggle for composure. "Dr. Finley, I really appreciate that you've taken the time to call me, but I've decided to leave this to fate. I've no desire to go through what I did the first time. If the lump is cancerous, then I don't intend to treat it. If it's not, then a year from now, I'll still be fine. Either way, I don't want to know. I'm through letting my life be ruled by some disease."

"Kara, I strongly advise against this. You're a healthy young woman with your whole life ahead of you. Even if you have a reoccurrence, we can more than likely pursue the same course of action. But you know that you don't have the luxury of time. I need you to come in for the biopsy tomorrow, so we know what we're dealing with. I'll work around your schedule if you tell me when a good time is for you."

I rub my throbbing temple wondering idly if maybe the cancer had spread to my brain now. I have been getting more headaches lately. "I'm sorry, Dr. Finley, but I'm afraid I've made up my mind. Thanks for calling." I still hear his protests as I end the call and hit the button to send any further calls to voicemail. I turn my chair back around toward my computer and notice someone standing just inches away. My hand flies to my chest as I gasp. "Uncle Lee, you scared me to death. I thought you were already gone."

He stares at me for a moment, before lowering himself into one of the chairs in front of my desk. *Shit, how much did he hear?* "What are you doing, Kara?" he asks, and I relax thinking we're talking business.

"I'm doing a spreadsheet to track the overhead in the South Carolina division. I think it's a good way to see why the expenses there have gone up—"

"I could give a fuck about that right now," he snaps. "I want to know why you're blowing your doctor off when obviously you have another lump. And I'm damn certain that my brother doesn't know about this because he's been far too calm. So since your secret is out and I'm not going to go away until you tell me everything, go ahead and get started." He makes a great show of settling back into his seat and placing his ankle over the knee of the other leg. I swear that as much as I love the man, I want to throw my stapler at him right now. I've seen that stubborn expression more times than I can count from my father, and I know if I attempt to get up and leave, he'll just chase me down. I open my mouth, but before I can speak he adds, "Oh, and don't bother lying. My bullshit detector is way better than my brother's."

Well, shit. I debate my options before finally giving up. He's got me. If I managed to get away, he'd probably bribe or threaten my doctor into revealing the truth anyway. So I admit, "I went for my recommended annual mammogram last week, and it showed a cyst in my breast—the other one. Due to my history, they want to do a needle biopsy to determine if it's cancerous." *I hate, absolutely hate, that these words are being spoken about my body again. I don't want to say or think the word biopsy, cysts, lumps, or anything else associated with the fucking nightmare of cancer.*

His face is impassive as he takes in my words. "All right, then why haven't you had that done yet? I assume your doctor wouldn't be calling you in the evening if you had."

"As I told my doctor, I don't intend to go through all of that again. I refuse to spend my life panicking over every little thing because I once had cancer."

My uncle flips a hand as if to say big deal. "So if it kills you, it does, right? No big thing."

I'm actually a little hurt by his nonchalance, but I try not to show it. "Exactly."

He studies his nails for a moment as the silence stretches between us. "You know I never pegged you for a coward. But what else can you call someone who buries their head in the sand when any type of diversity strikes?"

My mouth drops open as I stare at him in shock. I've been spoiled by my uncle my whole life. He's kissed my boo-boos, wiped my tears, and helped me talk my way out of trouble with my parents. He's a second father to me and has never talked to me the way he is right now. His disappointment literally flays me. "Bu—but you don't understand," I stutter out. "I—"

"That's where you're wrong, sweetheart. I've been places and done things that you could only imagine in your nightmares. I did whatever had to be done so your father and I could have a life. Yet you're playing with yours as if it's disposable. Maybe we all spoiled you too much, but we never wanted you or your brother to have to make the choices we did. Hell, the choices that my own daughter ended up making. What would have happened to Lia had she just decided to throw in the towel and say 'whatever' while she was living with an abusive mother and a monster for a stepfather? Instead, she fought back and clawed her way out. Yet you've been given everything and don't appreciate any of it." He lowers his voice as tears begin to dribble from my eyes. "I know you've had a tough time of it, kiddo, and it's done a real number on you. I was real proud of the way you faced your cancer and came out on the other side. And yes, your life is always going to be a bit different now because of the disease. But when you're dealt a shit hand, then you play that fucker for all you're worth. You don't sit there automatically assuming you've been defeated. The best times I've had have started out the worst."

He gets to his feet and opens his arms as he's done a thousand times before, and I'm on my feet snuggling against his chest in seconds. His familiar smell comforts me as I finally feel a crack in my armor. "I just want it all to be over," I sob against his expensive business shirt.

"Shhh, I know, sweetheart. But you have to face this. We're all here for you. You're not alone, and you never will be." He whispers more words of comfort until I'm down to the occasional hiccup. He grabs a handful of tissues from the box on my desk and pushes them in my hand as I move to sit in the chair next to the one he recently vacated.

"Are you going to tell Dad?" I ask, knowing that they rarely keep secrets from each other.

He puts a hand under my chin and wipes a stray tear away. "I'll give you a few days to do that yourself first. My brother and I don't keep secrets from each other, especially when they concern our children."

"Okay," I agree, already dreading what this will do to my parents. *Again.*

He surprises me by asking, "What happened to Aidan Spencer? You two were attached at the hip for a while, but I haven't seen him around lately." The shrewd look on his face says he suspects my apathy is tied to Aidan. My uncle is far too astute.

I shrug then get to my feet and begin putting the stuff on my desk away. "He couldn't deal with having a sick girlfriend. He's already lost too much."

I expect some kind of verbal attack against Aidan, but instead, my uncle simply says, "I see. Well, let's get out of here for the evening. How about a steak with your favorite uncle? I don't have any plans tonight, and I'm thinking you don't either." *What the hell? The iron man has nothing to say against Aidan? His defection of me doesn't bother him in the slightest?* Or are my antidepressants muting my feelings here?

I readily agree, wanting to prolong our time together. It actually feels good to be with someone who knows what's going on with me instead of hiding it. As we're leaving, I can't resist pointing out, "You know, you could take some of your own advice. Instead of being afraid of what will happen, you should call Liza and take a chance."

He gives me a rueful grin before ruffling my hair. "I guess no matter how old we are, there are still things in life that freak us the fuck out. You conquer your fears, and I'll work on mine. Deal?"

We shake hands, and I hope that he is better at keeping his vow than I am. Because even though my parents will soon know about the lump, I don't know if it changes anything. I'm functioning, and by all appearances, and with Jen taking on more, I am managing at work easily. But it's a hard slog. I don't feel as equipped or as sharp as normal, and I hate that. I'm still more tired mentally than I've ever been, and some days, I only want it to be over, regardless of how that happens.

CHAPTER FOURTEEN

Aidan

I'm just finishing a conference call when I hear a commotion outside my door. I disconnect the call and am getting to my feet when the door opens and Lee Jacks strolls in with my secretary right on his heels. "I'm sorry, Aidan, I couldn't stop him," she apologizes as she glares daggers at the other man.

"It's fine, Tricia. Why don't you go ahead and call it a day? I'll be leaving shortly myself." I eye Lee curiously, as she says good night and pulls the door closed behind her. Finally, I extend my hand across the desk, and he ignores it to take a seat. "Make yourself comfortable," I say sarcastically as I settle back in my chair. I've meet Lee a few times through the years at different social events, and now that Luc is married to his daughter, we see each other at family functions. Still, it's not in the norm for him to barge into my office. Plus, he looks a bit pissed off and *that* automatically puts me on my guard. I'm no pussy by any means, but Lee Jacks isn't exactly the type of man you want mad at you, especially when you have no idea why.

"Spencer, tell me why the fuck you dumped my niece? Because she gave me her version and it's fucking insane."

Did not see that one coming at all. He's here about Kara? "It's none of your business, Lee. Kara and I broke things off a few months ago. Why the sudden visit?"

He sits forward, and I swear to God, he looks as if he might leap over the desk for my throat. *What the fuck is going on here?* "I don't know if you're aware of it, but Kara is like another daughter to me. I love that kid dearly. So when I found out that she's decided to simply give up on life because of you, I took it rather hard. Plus, my brother and his wife are little more than basket cases now. Yet none of *our* begging, pleading, or threats are getting through to her."

I get to my feet so quickly my chair slams back against the wall. "Wait—what in the hell are you talking about?"

He stands as well, leaning his hands on my desk. "Had she not met you, asshole, she might be willing to do what's needed to save her life. Instead, she doesn't care anymore because she's too hung up on you. And apparently, if she can't have you, then she'd rather give up."

I couldn't give a shit who the man is now as I barrel around my desk and grab his shirt in my fist. "Start making some fucking sense before I kick your ass," I snarl. I've had it with this cryptic shit he's sprouting.

He shrugs out of my hold, and in a deadly calm voice, he says, "You'd better fucking mean it if you touch me again, boy. Sit your ass down and listen." I go to charge him, and he shakes his head and puts up a hand. "It's not going to help Kara if I put you in the hospital, and that's what's going to happen if you don't get it together and fucking listen."

I don't want to, but I back off. I'm not scared of him, but I'm missing something important here, and he has the answers. Instead, I sit on the corner of my desk and motion for him to continue.

"A few weeks ago, Kara went for her recommended yearly mammogram, and it showed a cyst in her other breast. Naturally, due to her previous battle with breast cancer, they wanted to do a biopsy right away, but she refused. She didn't intend to tell any of us about it, but I overheard her one evening talking to her doctor. I gave her a few days to tell her parents and thought that I'd gotten through to her. Well, she did tell them, but she still refuses to have the biopsy. Says she's not going to live her life in fear and doesn't want to know if it's cancer or not. She just carries on each day as if the threat isn't there. I swear to Christ if I hear her humming at her desk as if she doesn't have a care in the world one more time, I'm gonna lose it."

"FUCK," I hiss. "Why in the world would she do that? You can't just let something like that go. She's risking her life!" I get to my feet once again and pace my office. "You need to make her go; she has to have the biopsy. Why aren't you and her parents doing anything?" I shout.

I half expect him to pummel me, but he gives me a strange, satisfied half grin instead. "Believe me, we've tried. She's an adult, Spencer. Let's just hope it's not cancer because if it is, she might not be around much longer." *FUCK! NO!*

"That's not happening," I roar. "I'll find her, and if I have to carry her ass for that test, then I fucking will."

She can't. She can't just give up. She can't let the cancer win.

Mom let the cancer win and stopped fighting, and it tore my father and me apart. Time has not healed our hearts. We still miss her so dreadfully.

I can't let Kara do that to her family.

I can't let Kara do that . . . to me.

I'm halfway to the door when he says, "She moved out into her own place. Got tired of fighting with her parents. You might need the address." I'm vibrating with impatience while he takes a piece of paper off my desk and jots something on it before handing it over. Then he shocks me by pulling a key from his pocket and flipping it to me as well. "She works late most every night regardless of what I say. I own the building, so I'll have the doorman buzz you in. The rest is up to you, son."

I'm an absolute wreck as I follow the directions to the address Lee had written down. Kara might be sick again and isn't doing anything about it. Dear God, am I the reason she doesn't care? She may have gotten her family to back down, but that shit won't work with me. One way or another, I'll save her life because a world without her in it is one I don't care to be a part of. *Fuck! Fuck!*

Kara

It is almost nine by the time I fit the key in the door of my apartment. I've lived here for about a week now. It is a two-bedroom in a good neighborhood of Asheville. They usually have a long waiting list, but since my uncle owns the building, he managed to secure a unit that had just vacated. Of course, my parents weren't happy about it, but what could they say, really? I wasn't a child anymore, and it was the natural order of things to leave the nest.

I know they feel I moved because of our daily arguments over my continued refusal to have the biopsy, but that wasn't really it. While I was there, they couldn't make peace with my decision. I kept them in turmoil, and I didn't want that. Even my brother made a rare appearance the weekend before to tell me what a selfish bitch I was. Apparently, *my* desire regarding my health wasn't popular with anyone. Uncle Lee has been strangely silent on the subject lately, which is a little disarming. Maybe he finally understands, though, because he certainly isn't a man who ever let fear rule his life. Isn't that what I'm trying to do as well? Not be ruled by the unknown but, instead, take each day as it comes?

I lock the door behind me and walk straight to the refrigerator to get a bottle of water. Having had a late lunch means I'm not really hungry yet. I kick off my shoes and pad across the hardwood floors on my way to the bedroom. I almost reach the hallway when a lamp on a nearby table clicks on, and I see the outline of a man sitting on the sofa. When I scream, he moves quickly and clamps a hand over my mouth. "Princess, pipe down before someone calls the cops."

My eyes widen as I blink several times, thinking I'm hallucinating. "Aidan?" I whisper haltingly.

"If I move my hand, you're not going to start wailing again, right?" I nod, and suddenly, my mouth is free. "I've been here for hours," he grumbles. "Do you work this late every night?"

I nod, still staring at him. "Wh—what're you doing here in my apartment? How'd you get in?" *Oh, how I've missed him.* Despite the lethargy my antidepressants cause, my yearning for Aidan hasn't ceased. I've wanted it to cease. It hurts too much.

He reaches for a nearby switch and more light floods the room. He studies me then, as if he can see everything inside. "Fuck, you're beautiful," he says absently as he raises a finger to stroke my cheek.

I'm mesmerized for long moments by the naked desire I see in his eyes. I'm seconds away from doing something crazy like begging him to take me against the wall when my reason returns. I step away from his touch and put my hands on my hips. "I asked what you're doing here? I haven't seen or heard from you in months, so this is a bit of a surprise."

He releases a breath on a heavy sigh. "Come sit down and we'll talk." I want to tell him to get out, but my curiosity won't let me. What would make him break into my apartment and ambush me after all this time? There have been no calls, no texts, no nothing. So I perch on the cool leather surface several inches away from him and wait.

I'm not sure what I'm expecting, but when he blurts out, "I know about the biopsy," I almost fall on the floor.

Stunned, I whisper, "How? Only my parents and my uncle know about that."

"Lee came to see me earlier this evening. Actually, I think he came to kick my ass, but luckily, he changed his mind and gave me your key instead."

I can hardly fathom what he's saying. How dare Lee betray my privacy in this way and to Aidan of all people? I surge to my feet and point at the door. "Get out! He had no right to do that, and I don't care if you have a key or not. You broke into my home. I'll call the police if you don't leave immediately."

He puts his hands on my arms and shakes me slightly. "Stop it, Kara! Calm down and listen to me. You're not calling anyone, and I'm not leaving."

"Fuck you! Is this some kind of pity stop for you on the way to see your whore of the week? Did you agree to visit poor, disease-ridden Kara to alleviate your conscience? Maybe give her a push to have the stupid test, and when you fail, hey, at least you tried, right? You can walk away feeling better about yourself because that's what you're good at, right? Walking away before things get tough. Well, thank God you did in this instance. You were right all along. The clock was ticking, and it was just a matter of time before I got sick again. You must really feel like you dodged a bullet." My voice is so bitter I hardly recognize it. I see him flinch as my words hit their mark.

"Stop," he murmurs raggedly. When I don't, he curses under his breath and his lips cover mine roughly. I fight him for a moment, but then my body betrays me. I've never been able to resist him. He ravages my mouth before moving on to my neck. "I'm sorry, baby. I'm so fucking sorry," he repeats over and over, and he hugs me tightly to him. "I've been such an idiot, princess. Please don't make me live my life without you." Then I feel moisture. *Is he crying?*

"Aidan." I pull back. His eyes are wet and red as he meets my gaze. "What are you saying?" I ask, terrified that I'm misreading him.

"I love you, Kara, so much. That hasn't changed for one minute, and I've *barely* existed without you. I hope to God you can find it in you to forgive me for fucking this up so badly."

Confused, I say, "But nothing has changed. It may actually be worse, and you can't handle that. You'll leave me again," I say thickly, battling my own tears. I barely get those words out as a sob from deep within my heart escapes. *I wouldn't cope if he gave up on me again. I can't do that.*

He drops to his knees and puts his arms around my waist. "No, princess, fuck no. I'm not going anywhere. That was the biggest mistake I've ever made and that's saying something."

Almost as if they have their own will, my hands run through his hair, remembering—*loving*—the feel and texture of it. "Please don't tell me you're doing this so I'll have the biopsy. If this is something that you and my uncle cooked up—"

"For fuck's sake, Kara." He gets to his feet, looking angry. "I realize that you don't have a lot of reason to trust me right now, but give me more credit than that. You know damn well I'd never do that and neither would your uncle. Yes, hell yes, I want you to have the biopsy, and you bet your ass my reasons are selfish. I want you with me for a long time, and that means not taking any chances with your health. But—and believe me, I can't believe I'm saying this—it's your body, your life, and your choice. I may not agree with it, but I'll support whatever you decide because I'd expect the same from you. I'll absolutely let you know my feelings on it, but I will not leave you over it. I'll be right there by your side no matter which way you go."

I can hardly believe what I'm hearing, but I can't doubt the sincerity in his eyes. "You have no idea how much I want to hate you for what you've put us both through," I say tearfully. "Other than my family, you're the only man I've ever loved, and you let me down big time, buddy. I've turned myself into the most dedicated employee at Falco. I work twelve to fourteen hours a day, seven days a week, and then come home and collapse. That's the *only* way I've survived losing you, and it's never gotten any easier. I haven't coped, Aidan. My depression has come back . . . And I . . . I'm hurting and angry."

"I'm sorry, baby. I was so very wrong. Believe it or not, I pretty much came to that conclusion myself without your uncle threatening to kick my ass." I smile at that thought. My uncle can be terrifying when he's angry. *What did he say to Aidan?* Although, judging by what he just said, it wasn't about what Uncle Lee said. It was about Aidan's love for me. *I've been such an idiot, princess. Please don't make me live my life without you.* Yes, he's been an idiot, and I am barely holding on at the moment, but he loves me. And he thinks it's enough. I can't fathom my life without him in it. I've missed him so very much. Although I'm exhausted, I need him. I need his touch, his loving, his dominance. I've felt adrift without him. The surprise in his eyes as I begin to unbutton his dress shirt is almost comical. But this isn't funny. I *need* him.

"Um . . . princess, what's up?"

I look up briefly. "I need you to fuck me so I know that this is real, and you're here." When he continues to stare at me, I add impatiently, "A little help would be good right about now." That seems to spur him into action, and in almost a blink of an eye, we're both naked, and I'm in his arms. "You know I was thinking we could do this on the sofa or somewhere nearby. I haven't made my bed in days, so it's a bit messy."

I point at a nearby doorway, and he stumbles in the dark before laying me on the bed. Actually, part of my body is hanging off, but luckily, it's only my legs. He curses as he trips over something before locating the lamp and clicking it on. "Holy shit, babe, it's like an obstacle course in here. When's the last time you cleaned this floor? I think there might actually be a person buried under these shoes."

I roll my eyes and grab one of his legs. "If you're finished whining about my housekeeping, Martha Stewart, I have more pressing matters for you to take care of." I pause suddenly, wondering if he's been with another woman while we were apart. I look up at him with a question in my eyes, and he picks up on it immediately.

""No, princess. There has been no one else. I love you and only you." There's no doubting the sincerity of his words, and I feel an overwhelming sense of relief. His cock is bobbing just inches away from my mouth now, as if begging for my attention, and even though I'd like to tease him, I can't resist. So I wrap my hand around the base and lean forward to lick the tip. "Fuck yeah, princess," he hisses as my tongue laps at the pre-cum leaking from his slit. I finally take mercy on him and take as much of his length in my mouth as I can. I look up at him while I'm doing it because I know that drives him wild. He's pushing against the back of my throat and my eyes water as I try to ignore my gag reflex. I pump my hand up and down in tempo with my mouth, allowing my teeth to graze him on each thrust. "Suck me, baby, take it all," he cries as a flood of warm liquid shoots down the back of my throat. I struggle to swallow as stream after stream comes out. Dear God, the man has been saving this stuff up. When it's over, I suck on the sensitive head of his cock for a moment before releasing it with a pop.

I fully expect him to pounce on me now—because that's how it usually goes—so I'm surprised when he steps forward and scoops me in his arms once again before laying me down in the center of the bed. He crawls up next to me and lies down on his side. When I give him a questioning look, he runs a finger across my lips before trailing it down my neck. "We're always in such a hurry. I don't think I've ever taken the time to discover every inch of your gorgeous body. Hell, when you're naked, I lose my mind. But tonight, I want to make love to you. Let me worship you, beautiful, as you deserve to be."

What woman wouldn't melt at those words? A part of me wants to make a sarcastic quip because the intimacy of the moment is so intense, but I can't. He's showing me that this is a turning point for us, and I need to do the same. "I'd love that," I whisper as I relax. He kisses and touches my face and neck, not leaving an inch of skin undiscovered. But when he reaches my breasts, I freeze. He's touched me there before, but he didn't know then. I want to cover myself, to pull away and hide, but the look in his eyes stops me. I see understanding but no pity. I don't think I could have taken it had he felt sorry for me. His fingers are whisper light as he gently traces the contours of my reconstructed breast. He finds the tiny scars, and I flinch. Instead of the revulsion I feared to see on his face, nothing but love appears as he lowers his head and kisses the silvery lines. I feel tears trickle down my cheeks as he worships every part of my body. I'm panting and begging him to take me when he finally moves to join our bodies together. His fingers thread through mine as he makes love to me slowly and tenderly. "I love you, Aidan," I cry out as my orgasm washes over me.

"I love you too, princess," he groans as he finds his release as well. We stay joined for a long while, neither of us wanting to be apart. Finally, he leaves the bed to clean up and brings a warm cloth back to take care of me. I'm so tired that I manage to barely mumble my thanks. As I'm drifting off to sleep, I hear him whisper against the top of my head, "Please stay with me, princess." And I know that he's not talking about tonight. Little does he know that I made the decision to have the biopsy the moment I gave myself to him again. I can only pray that he hasn't given his heart to yet another woman who will leave him. *Not only do I not want to leave him, but I would hate to be the cause of more pain in this amazing man's life.*

CHAPTER FIFTEEN

Kara

Aidan's knee bounces rapidly as we wait for my name to be called at the radiologist's office. I'd phoned my doctor the next morning, and he managed to get me in right away. When I told Aidan my decision to have the biopsy, he'd been happy but also determined to be by my side every step of the way. I told him that my parents could accompany me, but he wouldn't hear of it. Truthfully, I was afraid that it would be too hard for him with his mother's death still so recent, but he assured me that he loved me and was with me no matter the pain it might cause him.

"Kara Jacks." Both Aidan and I flinch when the technician says my name. He gets to his feet first and gives me a bright smile. He puts his hand on the small of my back and directs me to where the nurse is waiting. She indicates a nearby door, and I enter behind her with Aidan on my heels. She gives me a paper gown and tells me to remove everything above the waist including any jewelry. Then I'm told to lie on a table where they'll use ultrasound to find the exact location of the lump and accurately insert a needle into it for the biopsy. "If you'll open your gown, we'll begin administering the local anesthesia," the nurse says. "You'll feel a pinch, but the area should numb quickly."

Aidan takes a seat on my other side and holds my hand in his. "I'm right here, princess," he assures me quietly. "Just look at me." He laughs softly as he says, "Remember that day in Charleston when you met my neighbor Brandy?"

I narrow my eyes at him, unable to believe he's going there now of all times. "Oh, I remember her," I huff. "Such a lovely young lady." I feel a twinge of pain as my breast is poked and prodded, but I'm too busy glaring at my boyfriend to pay it much attention.

"Admit it, baby, you were jealous. When I looked up and saw you coming down the beach, I thought you were going to mow down the poor girl. She was so generously offering to teach me to surf, and you were thinking of ways you could do her bodily harm."

"I so was not jealous. I didn't care at all that you were out there flaunting your abs for everyone to see. I mean, of course, you couldn't be bothered to put a shirt on before going to the beach. In a way, it was really your fault and not Brandy's."

"Oh, come on, princess." He laughs. "You knew even then that you were madly in love with me, and you were plotting to overthrow Brandy and steal me away." As I lie here sputtering indignantly, he winks and adds, "It's understandable, really. I am pretty hot, right?"

"Oh, my God," I say in amazement. "Could you possibly be any more vain? You're like the president and only member of your own fan club. I can't believe I'm in love with such an egomaniac. And for your information, I was nowhere near loving you back then. There was some lust involved—a lot of it—but that's it. Okay, maybe a few times I was confused about my feelings. I certainly liked you and thought it was possible that something was there. But with the kind of sex we were having, it was hard to be certain. Plus, with all the spankings you were giving me, it wasn't as if I had much of a chance to focus on the warm fuzzies. And let's not forget you tied me up several times—"

A throat clears nearby and then an amused male voice says, "I think we've got what we need, Kara."

I blink in surprise as I end my rant and become aware of my surroundings once again. *Oh, my God. What the hell have I been saying?* Aidan so skillfully sidetracked me that I completely focused on him and not what was happening. "I—you're already finished?" I ask in shock. The technicians assisting my doctor all appear to be fighting grins as they begin clearing their supplies away. I turn to Aidan, who is giving me a sheepish grin. "You did that on purpose, didn't you?"

It's impossible to be mad at him when he runs a finger down my cheek before helping me sit up and cover my breast once again. "I knew you were nervous and wanted to take your mind off what was happening."

"Thank you, babe," I say sincerely as I get to my feet and dress while he waits. The doctor says he'll have the results from the lab in a few days and that he'll give me a call. They give me the ice pack to prevent swelling and tell me to take it easy for the rest of the day. I didn't say what first popped into my mind: *"I know. Been there, done that."*

Soon, we're back in Aidan's car, and instead of going toward my office, we're heading in the opposite direction. When I question him, he takes my hand and raises it to his lips. "We're taking the day off so I can spend some time with my girl." I'm thrilled when we take the exit for Biltmore House, and he pulls into the long entrance.

I'm bouncing in my seat as I squeal, "I love it here! I can't believe we're doing this."

"I've never been, but I remember you mentioning it being one of your favorite places. So get ready to be my tour guide." A few minutes later, we're parked, and instead of taking one of the buses, we use a nearby path and walk to the house. It's just as beautiful and majestic as ever, and I find myself seeing it through new eyes as I show Aidan around. After we've spent several hours in the gorgeous Vanderbilt home, we walk through the gardens and find a private bench away from the crowds. I have my mouth full of the pastry we'd purchased from the outdoor bakery when Aidan suddenly drops to a knee in front of me with a velvet box perched on his open hand.

"What?" I mumble before I start coughing as the bite goes down the wrong way. He stands, thumping me on the back.

"Baby, are you okay?" he asks in concern as he hands me a water bottle.

I wave it away and look around frantically for the jewelry box I just saw. Surely, I didn't imagine that. When he doesn't say anything or make a move to return to his former position, I blurt out, "Was that a ring? I mean if it was, have you changed your mind? I'm not saying it was an engagement ring. It could have been a necklace." Although I'm not sure why he would give me another necklace. When he refastened the gorgeous heart pendant around my neck last night, I felt balanced somehow. *Cherished.* I squeeze my eyes shut before opening them again. "I know what I saw. It was real, right? Oh God, did you drop it when I choked?" I start to get to my feet when I realize he's bent over laughing.

"And that right there, princess, is one of the reasons I love you so much." Suddenly, the box is in his hand once again, and he flips the lid open to reveal a gorgeous princess cut diamond surrounded by smaller stones. It sparkles brightly in the midday sun as if motioning me closer. Aidan is on his knees for a second time as he removes the ring from the box. "Kara Jacks, I love you more than you'll ever know. I've come to realize that you're my soul mate and absolutely the one I was always meant to find. Please say you'll marry me and keep me on my toes and the edge of my seat for the rest of our lives."

I feel like I'm plunging a knife into my heart as I say, "But shouldn't we wait for the results? We don't know what's going to happen."

He slips the ring on my unresisting finger. "It doesn't matter what the test says. I vow to love and cherish you for the rest of our lives. Time has no meaning or place in those words. I'll love you until I die. In sickness and health, I'm here for you. Fuck the tests. Before Mom died, she told me something very true. Something I only understood because of you." He pauses, and I can see him struggling as he recalls her words. *He must miss her so much."* She said that I'll know the woman for me as she'll make me laugh, smile, and argue with passion. We do all of that, my beautiful Kara. That's how we love. Fuck the tests. We'll face any and everything together, and we'll do it as husband and wife."

"Yes," I cry, "my answer is yes a million times over." And in that magical garden where so many have walked before us, I pledge my heart and my life to the man who I once thought I could never have. And I finally understand that although cancer has taken so much from me, fate stepped in at just the right time and gave me back more than I could have ever imagined. I have no idea what tomorrow will bring and how long we have together, but I'll no longer allow my fear to keep me from living my life to the fullest with the one man who pushed away the dark and brought me into the light.

The End

EPILOGUE

Aidan

I smile like the besotted sap I am as Kara runs toward the finish line. She's dressed in pink, as are the other participants competing in the fun run to raise money for breast cancer research. After her biopsy results came back negative, we'd both been overcome with relief. But it also ignited something inside her. Instead of standing fearfully on the sidelines, she is now determined to do all she can to spread the word about early detection and yearly mammograms before the age that most doctors recommend. When she told Lee she wanted to organize a yearly charity benefit with Falco Industries as the sponsor, he'd been completely on board. I also discussed it with Lucian who'd been more than happy to add Quinn Software as an additional sponsor. This first event had raised over fifty thousand dollars for the Hope Women's Cancer Center with additional funds pledged in the future.

She comes running straight for me after crossing the finish line, and I swing her up in my arms before twirling her around. "You were amazing, baby." I smile. "Plus this sweaty body is doing big things for me."

"Is that so?" She grins as she rubs against me.

"Better be careful, princess. Your dad is glaring at me. Unless you want to lose a part of my body that you're really fond of, you need to cease and desist."

She giggles before allowing me to put a few inches of space between us. "I'm beat." She grimaces as I hand her the bottle of water I grabbed earlier.

"I'm proud of you. You worked your ass off on this." I'm kissing the tip of her nose when I see the last person cross the finish line. I look away only to jerk right back. "Oh no," I whisper disbelievingly. "How—"

She gives me an innocent look that I know is complete bullshit. Then I spot Lucian shaking his head as he stands beside a grinning Lia. "I thought Misty was a good friend of yours." Kara giggles.

"Aidan! Is that you, sugar?" Misty is bearing down on us now, and I panic.

I grab Kara's hand and start running. She's trying to protest but laughing too much to be coherent. "If you love me at all, you'll move your ass." Then we're sprinting for my car as we ignore Misty's shrill cries for me to stop. As my gorgeous fiancée jumps in the car and I slide around the front, it hits me. My mother was absolutely right. The one who makes me laugh, smile, and even argue with passion *is* absolutely the love of my life and the one I am meant to be with for all time. And I firmly believe she is looking down at me right now because there's no way Heaven could ever keep her from getting the satisfaction of knowing she was right all along.

ALSO BY SYDNEY LANDON

The Danvers Novels
Weekends Required
Not Planning on You
Fall For Me
Fighting For You
Betting on You (A Danvers Novella)
No Denying You
Always Loving You
Watch Over Me
The One For Me
Wishing For You (11/1/2016)

The Pierced Series
Pierced
Fractured
Mended
Rose
Aidan

Coming November 1, 2016
The last book in the Danvers series,
Wishing For Us
Available NOW for pre-order.
Please turn the page for a special excerpt.

CHAPTER ONE

The relentless pounding in her head was what finally woke Lydia Cross from a sound sleep. Her mouth felt like she had been chewing on a dirty gym sock and her eyes were glued together so tightly it took several attempts for her to pry them open. She lay in a darkened room, attempting to get her bearings. A quick glance at the clock on the bedside table had her sitting up too quickly—which turned out to be a big mistake. Her stomach immediately staged a revolt and she struggled to free herself from under the covers—then promptly smacked into a hard surface. *What the hell?* Who'd moved the wall in her bedroom? She rubbed her smarting nose and inched along with half-closed eyes until she reached a doorway. She fumbled before locating the light switch and flipped it up. The bright glare that filled the unfamiliar bathroom temporarily blinded her.

After blinking a few times, she was able to focus on her surroundings. Then it finally hit her that she was in Vegas. Her co-worker and good friend, Crystal Webber, was getting married to Mark DeSanto in a few days and their friend, Mia Gentry, had insisted on throwing the bachelorette party at the Oceanix-Las Vegas. Luckily, Danvers was a big company and temporary replacements could be found so they could take a few days of vacation together with no problem.

The nausea that had temporarily abated while she was hunting for the bathroom returned in full force. She barely made it to the toilet before the contents of her stomach came back up in horrifying fashion. She was doing her best to remain upright when her hair was suddenly pulled back and someone touched her back. She jerked in shock, nearly falling into the toilet, before strong hands steadied her. A masculine voice rumbled, "It's okay, little one. I've got you."

Lydia managed to shrug out of the hold long enough to spin around and look at her mystery bathroom guest. "Sweet Jesus," she exclaimed at the sight of Jacob Hay, clad only in snug boxer briefs, towering over her with concern etched on his face. She couldn't help herself—she drank him in from head to toe. Who in the world could possibly blame her for taking advantage of this screwed-up nightmare to check out the man she'd lusted after for months? In all her fantasies, though, she'd never quite imagined him in this scenario. "Wh—what are you doing here?" she asked in confusion, before belatedly realizing that she was also quite naked. She grabbed a robe off a nearby hook and fumbled to put it on.

Jacob raised an amused brow at her. "After last night, I wouldn't have guessed that you had a shy bone in your body, gorgeous."

Oh shit, what's he talking about? Did I wrap myself around him and beg him to come to my room? "You've got three seconds to tell me what in the hell you're doing in my hotel room," she snapped. Thank God, she'd finally gotten the damn robe tied. Laying down the law was rather hard when your boobs were hanging out.

Instead of answering right away, Jacob walked calmly around her and flushed the toilet. He then moved to the sink, unwrapped a toothbrush, and filled a glass with water. He motioned her over and she flushed as she realized he was trying to get her to brush her teeth. Maybe she could pause for a moment to take care of her breath before she continued her inquisition. Lydia quickly took care of business before putting her hands on her hips. "Well?"

He looked as if he was biting back a smile. "Could we possibly take this conversation into the next room?"

She resisted the urge to childishly stomp her feet as once again, he made her feel like an idiot. Naturally, he didn't want to stand around and chat in the room she'd just tossed her cookies in. "Oh, all right," she grumbled as she stalked past him. *Wait, I don't remember my room being this nice.*

He moved over to the bedside table and picked up the phone. Despite her glare, he calmly placed an order for coffee and Danishes from room service. Then he turned back to face her. *So hot,* she thought to herself. He studied her for long enough that she began to fidget. When he finally spoke, the deep rumble of his voice in the quiet room had her jerking. "Do you not remember anything about last night?"

Was he nuts? Would she be standing here looking like a complete train wreck if she knew what was going on? But instead of opening her mouth to unleash a sarcastic comment, she took a breath and admitted, "I have no idea. I vaguely remember going dancing at some club with Mia and Crystal." She rubbed her throbbing temple as she attempted to recreate the events of the previous evening. "Didn't Mark and some of his friends show up at some point?"

He had the look of a proud teacher as he nodded his head encouragingly. "That's right. I flew here with Mark and the Jackson brothers. We met up with you ladies sometime during your club crawl."

Images exploded in her head as jumbled memories came rushing back to her. *Dancing. The taste of his lips. Our tongues tangling. Hands touching. My new husband.* Wait, what? Lydia stared at Jacob in dawning horror before looking down at the glittering diamond on her ring finger.

Holy. Fucking. Shit.

"We got married," she whispered, then promptly staggered over to the bed and dropped down onto it.

***

Just the reaction every man hopes to see from his new bride, Jacob thought as he took in Lydia's shocked demeanor.

He sat down on the side of the bed and held her hand. He placed a few fingers on her forehead and caressed her gently, asking, "Feeling better?" He had no idea why he was checking her for signs of a fever when he knew it was the alcohol and shock that had gotten to her.

Her earlier panic seemed to have receded, leaving a look of helpless confusion in its place. "Did we really...get married? I'm imagining that whole thing, right?"

She looked so hopeful that he hated to burst her bubble, but he couldn't lie to her. He rubbed what he hoped was a soothing pattern on the back of her hand, as he said, "No, it actually happened. The king himself performed the ceremony."

"The king?" A helpless giggle escaped her luscious lips. "That's right... We were married by Elvis Presley—or, at least, someone loosely resembling him. God, I still remember the— *'thank you...thank you very much.'*"

Jacob found himself laughing along with her. At thirty-four years old he had just gotten married in Vegas by a terrible Elvis impersonator. And to top it off, his new bride was all but a stranger to him. Hadn't his mother preached to him and his brother about impulse control from the time they were small? Clearly he'd completely lost his mind last night. Hell, he'd known it was wrong, but when Lydia looked at him all teary eyed and—

She pulled her hand out from under his and ran it through her sexy, tousled hair. Her large green eyes locked on his, and he found himself swallowing hard. *So damn beautiful.* "I recall pieces of the evening, but not what led up to our—union. Why would we have done something like that? Do you remember anything?"

***

Before he could answer, there was a knock at the door. "That'll be room service." Lydia pulled the sheet up to her neck and cowered as Jacob sauntered toward the door, seemingly not the least bit concerned that he wore only a pair of very revealing underwear. Of course, what did he have to be embarrassed about? His body was chiseled perfection. Broad shoulders and a muscular chest, abs that looked like they belonged on an underwear advertisement, tapering into lean hips and a bulge between his thighs that had her mouth watering.

Hells bells. She was married to Jacob Hay.

It was so unfair that she couldn't remember every detail of the previous night in vivid color. If there were a God, it would come back to her. She was freaked out over the state of things this morning, sure, but the real tragedy was not knowing exactly how it felt to be bedded by—

"Lydia."

Her head snapped up as she noticed the object of her drool fest standing before her with his hands on his hips. *Please, no, don't put your cock at eye level with me.*

"Are you all right? I called your name several times, but you weren't responding." He looked at her in concern, probably noticing her dilated pupils and the way her eyes were glued to his package.

Guess what, Jacob? Your new wife is a pervert.

"Um—I." She cleared her throat and tried again. "I'm fine. Just tired, I guess." Pointing at the table across the room that now held a carafe, she quickly asked, "Could I have some coffee?" She was sure he wondered why she couldn't get it, but she needed a moment to compose herself and get her libido back under control. With that thought, she tried to sound casual as she tossed out, "If you want to get dressed first, that's okay. You must be—cold."

When he turned to stare at her questioningly, she caught sight of something she'd missed. *Because you couldn't stop looking down long enough to see anything above the waistband.* Jacob's neck and chest had scratch marks and what looked like bites all over them.

No...she couldn't have. She'd never been that aggressive in bed. Surely, it was from an interlude with someone else that preceded her night with him.

He followed her line of sight, and then his lips curled up into a devilish smile. His eyes blazed with heat and she felt her core clenching in response. "For such a little thing, you pack quite a punch, sweetheart."

Sweet baby Jesus. She felt her mouth opening and closing without a sound as she took in the damage she'd inflicted on him. Had she thought the man was a chew toy or something? Those indentions weren't made by one little nibble. No, she'd obviously attacked his chest and nipples like a rabid dog. She was relieved that his boxer briefs outlined his dick so clearly now. At least that was proof she hadn't bitten off the sucker. She put a hand over her face before mumbling, "Stuff like this doesn't happen to me. I've never even gone down on a guy!"

She continued to toss out all of the reasons that the last twenty-four hours were unbelievable, but a hand on her leg had her pausing to look up at a more serious Jacob. "What?" she asked, strangely unnerved that he no longer looked amused by their circumstances.

Clearly it was finally dawning on him that he'd married her. The poor man was probably about to weep at his misfortune. She'd surely marked his body for life.

"You've never performed oral sex?" Jacob asked, sounding strangled.

Removing his hand, Lydia could only gawk at him. Finally, she managed to ask, "Out of everything I just said, that's what you're focused on?" *Over-share much?* Why in the world would she have blurted out something so personal to him? Granted, apparently he was her new hubby, but still… When he continued to stare at her, she added, "It just never came up, okay?"

Really poor choice of words, Lydia. Now, she was stuttering as she went into more unnecessary explanations. "My fiancé, Brett, didn't really enjoy the whole—oral aspect and he was my one and only, so—"

"You've only had sex with one man before last night?" Jacob croaked out. Lydia gave a squeak of surprise when he flopped down on the bottom of the bed, barely missing her toes. He lay on his back, staring up at the ceiling as if it contained answers to some of the questions that must be running on a loop through his mind. She wanted to mention again that he could put some clothes on, but truthfully, a nearly nude Jacob wasn't exactly a hardship. Their conversation was becoming more and more surreal. She didn't even know him well enough to consider him a casual acquaintance. He was her man crush, and she enjoyed objectifying him anytime she caught a glimpse of him in the hallways of Danvers Inc, thinking that there was no harm in entertaining herself with the fantasies.

The only time she could remember actually carrying on a conversation with him was when he'd helped her in the parking garage at the office once when her car wouldn't start. Yet somehow, she'd married him last night and then gone ahead and had what was probably mind-blowing sex to top it off. *Am I upset because we're hitched or because I don't remember my night in bed with him?*

In a voice laden with sarcasm, she said, "If we could possibly step back from my sexual history for a moment, I'd like to discuss a more important matter here. You seem far more knowledgeable about last night than I am. So could you please tell me what led to finding myself married to you this morning?"

A quick peek toward the foot of the bed showed Jacob's washboard abs rippling as he scrubbed his hands over his face. *Look away, girl, he's not really yours.* His voice was deep and gravelly when he began explaining. "You said that you remember Mark showing up last night." She nodded her head, and he continued. "Mark and I were in San Francisco. I guess when he spoke with Crystal, he decided to take a detour and visit her. I told him it was fine with me. I'd planned to get a room and crash for the night. Asher and Dylan Jackson were here on business since their family owns the Oceanix Resorts, so I ended up having a drink with them. I ran into you in the hallway outside the bathrooms."

"And you actually recognized me?" she couldn't help but ask.

"Of course," he said, sounding slightly offended. "You're not an easy woman to forget, Lydia, trust me on that." She tried her best not to melt into a warm puddle at his words. She'd have been thrilled had he just admitted she looked vaguely familiar. "Anyway, we chatted for a few moments, and I walked you back to the table where your friends were. It was pretty late by that point and most of the ladies were in the process of leaving. Within a couple minutes, only you and I were left. So we had a few more drinks and talked. In hindsight, we probably should have switched to water, but that didn't happen."

Lydia pinched the bridge of her nose before saying, "I still don't see how we got from there to Elvis marrying us. I've had a few drinks before without marrying the first man I ran into."

She yelped as Jacob pinched her toe. "Thanks for the ego boost, sweetheart. You make it sound as if you tied the knot with the casino janitor."

"This is no time to get sensitive," she chided, although she did feel a little guilty for the unlikely possibility that she had in fact hurt his feelings. Her opinion wouldn't keep a man like Jacob up at night.

His hand remained on her foot, and strangely enough, he began rubbing it absentmindedly. She wondered if he was aware he was even doing it. "You told me about your fiancé's death and how sad you were that you'd never have your happily ever after like Crystal and Mark."

"Oh good Lord." Lydia sagged back against the mattress, feeling boneless in her embarrassment. Maybe the bed would swallow her up and she could end this misery now. She'd literally been crying in her beer in front of the man she fantasized licking like a Popsicle. *Color me pathetic.* "And you what, took pity on me and decided to help me mark a big one off my bucket list?"

The hand on her foot froze as he said, "It really wasn't like that, Lydia. We really connected and got swept up in the moment together. I could see that you were still in pain, even though it's been three years since Brett died. You had a life planned with him and then it was taken away from you. Naturally, you would feel that loss keenly at an engagement party. You showed no sign of being jealous of Crystal and Mark. You were just sad that the wedding you'd planned never came to be. So even though you were joking when you asked me to marry you, I said yes. Then we took a cab a few blocks to the wedding chapel and made it official."

It was worse—so much worse—than she had even imagined. "Jacob," she began hoarsely once she could speak past the lump in her throat, "I—I don't know what to say. You didn't have to marry me last night just because you pitied me. And I can't believe I went along with it. Was I coherent when I said, 'I do?'"

She squealed in alarm when Jacob suddenly shifted to his knees, and in a blur of movement that her eyes could hardly track, he was straddling her body. He looked beyond pissed when he gritted out, "Let's get a few things straight. First off, I didn't marry you because I felt sorry for you. Get that out of your head right now. Did I feel bad that you'd lost your fiancé? Hell, yeah. I'm only human. But your strength really struck me last night, Lydia. You were so damned happy that your friend had found Mark and there wasn't a trace of pettiness behind it. You told me about sitting with Brett in his last days and doing everything short of moving mountains to make all of his last wishes come true. It was clear to me that you could have given up and walked away, but you stayed with him until the end. You're strong and selfless. So when I asked you what your dream was and you said to get married the way that you'd planned, something came over me, Lydia...I wanted to give it to you. It may be crazy, but I had no reservations when I gave you my name."

Lydia was riveted as she stared up at him. The truth of his words was plain to see in his body language. She'd told him everything about Brett's death; otherwise, he'd never have known all the details he'd so achingly replayed for her. She could feel her bottom lip tremble as tears welled in her eyes. "But we're strangers," she whispered. "Before last night, the only thing I really knew about you was that you were handy with a spare tire and worked for Mark DeSanto. And I'm sure you knew even less about me."

Jacob lowered his hand to gently trace the curve of her mouth. "I desired you from the moment you stood before me in that silky white dress in the garage, looking like the most beautiful damsel in distress I'd ever seen. I'm surprised you didn't notice what a fumbling mess I was while I was working on your car. I wanted to ask you out that day, but—well, things were so damned complicated in my life then, and I thought you deserved a man who could devote all of his attention to you."

"That wasn't that long ago," she pointed out. "What's changed for you since then?"

He opened his mouth and then closed it again. Finally, he shrugged and said, "Maybe I just didn't want to miss my chance with you. Sooner or later, someone would come along and sweep you off your feet and I'd have kicked myself that I'd let you go without getting a shot."

She felt dazed as she considered his words. Had he really been that attracted to her from their first meeting? That would mean that he'd felt at least some of what she had after the time they'd spent together that day.

He pointed toward the bed then asked in a hesitant voice, "Do you remember anything that happened here afterward?"

Lydia felt heat rush into her cheeks. Bits and pieces of the time she'd been in his arms were steadily coming back to her. There were gaps, but the longer she was awake, the more she remembered. *Thank God.* She would likely have never gotten over forgetting her first time with Jacob. "Not all of it," she admitted. "But...I know you, um, were on top, then I was, and then your mouth... Any other times that I'm missing?"

Sounding strained, he said gruffly, "No, baby, I think that about covers it. Thank fuck." He ran an unsteady hand through his thick, dark hair. "Last night was...special to me. And it was going to suck if you didn't have any recollection of it."

She put a hand over his and squeezed. "I know how it felt, Jacob. I was really confused when I woke this morning. I'm guessing both from the alcohol and a lack of sleep. But things are starting to come back to me." Her eyes darted down as she added, "You made me feel cherished. You held me as if I was someone that you cared about. I haven't had that in a long time. With the chemo and his illness, Brett was unable to—you know, so…"

"I understand," he said softly. He shifted to the side. Lydia was mourning the loss of their body contact when he rolled her into his arms.

She snuggled against him, loving the musky, masculine smell of his body. "What now?" She hoped he didn't detect the hint of misery in her voice. They were strangers who had married in a moment of temporary madness. The only thing to do was to have the marriage dissolved and move on.

The sad thing was, they had been together for less than a day, but she knew that she'd miss him dreadfully when he was gone. But since he'd done what he thought she needed last night, now she would be strong and return the favor by giving him his freedom without any hassle. "Can we get an annulment since we've—you know, slept together? Does a drunk Elvis wedding really count as a legal marriage?"

Jacob's chest rumbled under her ear as he laughed. She felt something press against the top of her head, but surely he wouldn't have kissed her, would he? That would be a gesture of affection, and they barely knew each other. "I don't know the particulars of a Vegas wedding, sweetheart, but it's nothing we need to worry about right now. No need to rush into anything without thinking it through."

She rolled her eyes, even though she knew he couldn't see her. "I think the ship has already sailed on the whole rushing into things, wouldn't you say?"

"Sure," he agreed easily. "Maybe what I should have said was that we don't have to make any decisions right now. We'll figure things out once we get home and the dust has settled. Today, we'll fly home together and go from there."

"But I'm supposed to travel back with the girls at nine." She flipped over to look at the bedside clock then shrieked quite loudly in Jacob's ear. "Dammit! It's past that time now! Why didn't they call or come by my room? I can't believe they would just leave me here."

She was on the verge of a full freak out when Jacob calmly announced, "You're flying home with me on Mark's plane. He and Crystal are staying an extra day, so we'll go back today and then I'll send the jet back for them. We're leaving at noon, so we have plenty of time to dress and have breakfast before the car picks us up."

I'm lying with scantily clad Jacob Hay calmly discussing cars and jets. Someone needed to pitch her and bring her back to reality. Even as Lydia pondered how bizarre the morning had been, she couldn't help but marvel at how well she was handling it all.

It's not as if something like this had ever happened to her before. So why wasn't she having some kind of panic attack? Delayed reaction? Possibly some kind of trauma-induced shock? She thought it was more likely that she didn't want the dream to end. Heck, just a few days ago, she would have bet money that she'd never even enjoy a first date with Jacob. Now, she was cuddled in his strong arms and it felt almost natural—as if she belonged there, which was absolutely nuts. She shifted slightly, moving her hand and froze. Oh God, the ring. How could she have forgotten about that? Was it real? It certainly looked as if it was. And it was easily two carats, maybe more, and there were more diamonds in the matching wedding band. Extending her arm, she wiggled her finger and asked, "Where did this come from?"

He gave a lazy laugh before putting his hand next to hers. A wide, silver band adorned his finger. She gasped in surprise. "It came from the same jewelry store that this one came from."

Clearing her throat, she asked, "Was it expensive? How much does a sterling silver ring cost? Can we return it all?"

"You're pretty cute when you ramble." He chuckled. "Our rings are platinum, not silver, so no, they weren't exactly cheap. As I said earlier, I don't think we should concern ourselves with anything major right now, so let's not rush out and pawn anything, okay?"

Stunned, Lydia asked, "But why would you buy something so expensive when you knew it wasn't a real wedding?"

He looked uncomfortable as she stared down at him. Finally, he shrugged and said, "We've both acknowledged that we had a bit too much to drink last night. I'm sure neither of us was thinking clearly. It obviously seemed like the right thing to do at the time."

She opened her mouth to question him further when a nearby phone began ringing. He shifted their weight until he could look at the screen on the nearby bedside table. She thought she saw him wince before he said, "I've got to take this. Why don't you go shower and dress?"

You've been dismissed.

Before she could move, he answered the call with a, "Just a second," then appeared to be waiting for her to move. She scrambled off his chest and out of the bed with the grace of a dancing elephant. "I'll, um—just be in the bathroom."

As she was hurrying into the other room, she heard him say, "What do you need, Chris?"

Chris? That was a man's name, right? Why had he made such a point to get rid of her if he was just taking a business call or even one from his buddy? She'd had the distinct feeling it was a woman, but there had been no affection in his voice. Actually, he'd sounded cold—as if he didn't like the person on the other end of the line.

Lydia started the shower, and then dropped her robe onto the floor. The mirror showed marks on her body as well, but Jacob had still gotten the worst of it. Hers looked more like whisker burns. Then her nipples hardened involuntarily as pieces of her night with Jacob played in her head. She had hazy recollections of his mouth on her body—and dear God, between her legs. As her clit started to throb, she wanted nothing more than to march back into the bedroom and beg him to ravish her again, this time while she was sober. It seemed like a crime that she couldn't recall every moment. When a knock sounded at the door, she jumped backward, narrowly avoiding a nasty fall. "Er—yes?" she called out. *I sound guilty, as if I were in here thinking of sex—and him.*

"Everything okay? I thought I heard you say something." Geez, had she actually been in here moaning while thinking of last night? She needed to do some damage control—fast. "Mmm, no. I was just…singing in the shower." Lydia cringed at her lie. Couldn't she have come up with something better than that?

There was silence for a moment before he came back with, "What song?"

Are you kidding me? Who in the hell carried on a conversation about something so mundane through the bathroom door? It was almost as if he knew she was lying and was trying to make her squirm. *"Fight Song."* She blurted out the last thing she could remember singing. She doubted he knew the empowerment song, but hopefully, it would satisfy his curiosity enough to get him to go away.

"Really?" he mused. "I like that one. Carry on with whatever you were doing then."

Lydia wasted no time getting in the shower and shutting the door behind her. Within a few minutes, she was finished and drying off with one of the hotels fluffy towels. She wrapped another around her hair before dressing in her robe once again.

When she opened the door and stepped out into the room, he gave her a leisurely once-over before walking toward the bathroom. "Do you have any idea where my luggage and purse are?" she asked, looking around the room.

"Everything should be on the other side of the bed. I found your room key and grabbed your stuff while you were showering. Let me know if I missed anything."

The next few hours passed in a blur. After they had both dressed, they opted for breakfast in the restaurant downstairs while waiting for the car to pick them up for the airport. Lydia stared at the passing scenery in a daze. She could barely fathom what had occurred during her girls' weekend in Vegas.

She'd assumed Jacob would be rushing her toward divorce court with embarrassing haste, but instead, he changed the subject or brushed off her concerns when she brought it up. Finally, she'd stopped trying and decided to enjoy the brief moment as a married woman. After all, in the real world, a man like Jacob Hay was about as likely to walk through her door as the Easter Bunny.